THE
English
Murder

A Mistake That Went Viral, A Life That Fell Apart

Sumit Goyal

 Scribe

The English Murder

Copyright © 2025 Sumit Goyal

Publisher: Inkscribe Publishing Pvt. Ltd

ISBN Number: 978-1-966421-71-9

CONTENTS

CHAPTER 1

THE TWEET THAT SHOOK A NATION

If anyone had told Rajeev Yadav that democracy in India would tremble because of three pegs of cheap whiskey and one mistyped tweet, he would've laughed and said, "Don't be stress, be progress!"

But fate, like Rajeev's English, had a wicked sense of humor.

It all started at Simran's house — the unofficial headquarters of The Chai Chronicles.

She had baked a gigantic cake with "Family Forever" written in sloppy pink icing. No real occasion. Just "life celebration," she said, beaming, like she was about to award them all lifetime achievement awards in friendship.

The living room was alive with music and fairy lights. Someone had strung up a random "Happy Birthday" banner because "Fun's the goal, not the role," Meher declared, already two beedis in and humming along to an old Lucky Ali song.

Kabir lounged on a bean bag, fiddling with his camera, angling it just right to catch the glow on Meher's face.

Rohan scrolled through work emails guiltily, hoodie pulled over his head like a monk trying to avoid temptation.

Zayan, as usual, was balancing a shot glass on his forehead, declaring, "Physics is an illusion created by sober people."

And in the middle of it all —

Rajeev Yadav, in a red checked shirt two sizes too bright, was making everyone laugh so hard that Simran's pet goldfish looked stressed.

"I am telling you," Rajeev declared, waving a samosa like a mic, "in my childhood, I was very... 'prestigious' in English speaking. Just my tongue had network problem."

Laughter exploded.

For a brief second—before the music roared back and someone tossed a pillow at Zayan—Rajeev's smile faltered.

His mind, traitorous and cruel, tugged open an old memory: sitting in a sweaty classroom, second bench from the front, the teacher reading out his essay and wheezing, "My aim is to becoming a Prime Minister because mango is my favouritest fruit."

Laughter. That sharp, echoing kind. Not with you—at you.

He'd laughed too, of course. Always first to laugh at himself. That was the trick, wasn't it? If you made it a joke before they did, it hurt a little less.

Maybe that's why, years later, when the UPSC prelims list came out and his roll number was missing like it owed someone money, he just renamed the PDF "Epic Failures" and never spoke of it again.

"Prestigious! Network problem!" Zayan choked out between gasps.

Even Aarushi — the unshakeable, always-composed Aarushi — let out a short, startled laugh. The kind of laugh you try to hide but can't.

And that's when Rajeev looked at her. Really looked.

Something tilted inside him—gentle yet inevitable—like the earth leaning a fraction closer to the sun. As if every feeling of love within him surged into tidal waves, rising with quiet force, only to break softly against the fragile shores of his innocent heart.

Aarushi stood near the window, glass of Coke in hand, her lawyer-sharp mind temporarily offline. Her hair was messy from the humidity, and she wore an old Kurti with faded denims — a far cry from her usual power suits.

She caught Rajeev staring and raised an eyebrow in mock threat. 'Say prestigious one more time, and I'll file a PIL against your vocabulary. Mind my words—someone will do that someday.

Rajeev grinned. Wide. Unfiltered.

"Permission to fall in love granted, Milord?" he said dramatically, hand to heart. The group howled.

Aarushi shook her head, smiling despite herself.

"You'll need to file an affidavit for that nonsense, Mr. Yadav."

Simran squealed, Kabir clicked rapid photos, and Meher shouted, " Well, well, legal romance brewing!"

Rajeev bowed clumsily, knocking over a bowl of chips.

Everyone clapped like it was a stage play, and for a minute, the world outside — the bills, the headlines, the judgmental relatives — disappeared.

In that cozy, chaotic room—filled with bad jokes and even better people—Rajeev felt something he hadn't felt in years: invincible.

Fears, after all, don't live outside us—they grow in the shadows of our own hearts and minds, fed by our silence and surrender.

For Rajeev, the greatest fear wasn't rejection. It was carrying the weight of unspoken love for Aarushi forever.

One-sided love, when stretched over time, transforms—the need for a response fades, and all that remains is the aching need to speak your truth, just once.

That night, the whisky quieted his inner ghosts, but it wasn't the alcohol that gave him courage. He fought and finally, he won.

Hours slipped by, each second steeped in the quiet bliss of friendship and the unspoken warmth of love that lingered in the air.

The playlist shifted from 90s Bollywood to random Punjabi remixes. Empty soda cans stacked into pyramids.

Arguments broke out over the right pronunciation of "quinoa."

By midnight, Simran had fallen asleep mid-conversation with a cupcake in her hand. Rohan was quietly setting up makeshift beds with cushions and old bedsheets.

Kabir and Meher had wandered out to the small iron-grilled balcony, where the noise of the party thinned out and the night's stillness took over.

A string of dim fairy lights blinked like slow heartbeats, casting their shadows against the peeling wall. Above them, the sky stretched out like a question nobody knew how to answer.

"The stars look... existential tonight," Kabir murmured, his camera hanging loose around his neck, unused for once.

Meher took a drag of her beedi and blew the smoke upward, letting it blur the cosmos. "That's because they're dead," she replied dryly. "What you're seeing is ancient light. They've already exploded. But we still romanticize the sparkle."

Kabir half-smiled, watching her outline glow faintly in the moonlight. "So basically, stars are like exes. Dead, distant, but somehow still messing with your timeline."

Meher chuckled. "Damn. Post that on your Instagram and get ready for 700 likes and three DMs from sad poets."

Inside, Zayan had just grabbed Rajeev's phone without asking, grinning like a teenager with a mission. "Bhai, I'm doing it," he whispered dramatically. "Calling my ex. Let's see if she still picks up when destiny dials."

"Which one?" asked Simran, peeking over his shoulder.

"The one who broke my heart but not my password," Zayan grinned.

He tapped, waited, and held his breath.

No answer.

He tried again.

Still nothing.

"Beta, stars might be dead, but exes? They're just on 'Do Not Disturb,'" Kabir called out from the balcony.

The group burst into laughter.

Meher, however, stared at the sky just a second longer — like she was asking it something it refused to answer.

And Rajeev... Rajeev stood on Simran's rooftop—phone in one hand, heart in the other. The screen glowed with cold light, while his heart pounded with the heat of everything he'd never said.

Three pegs down.

Slightly heroic.

Very, very loud inside his own head.

As he scrolled past the chaos—protests blazing, politicians roaring, the nation simmering—something stirred within him. The love in his chest didn't vanish; it transformed.

For the first time in a long while, he felt heard—and in that moment, he wished for every silenced voice in the country to echo just as loud, just as clear.

Rajeev, in his gloriously messed-up English and even more gloriously big heart, thought:

"No. I will say something good. Something brave."

So, he clicked "compose tweet." Thumbs fumbling. Spirit soaring.

And he wrote:

@ProudRajeev95:

This country needs a proper erection not this dicktaker ship. Jai Hindi. 2:12 AM · Twitter for Android

He read it twice. Nodded to himself. Felt like patriot with a smartphone.

Then he locked his phone, patted his chest proudly, and whispered, "Revolution initiated, baby."

Below the rooftop, the world slept. The stars blinked indifferently. Somewhere in the distance, a stray dog barked at nothing (or perhaps at some unseen chaos about to unfold.

And on the great spinning chaos of the internet, the tweet — ridiculous, heartfelt, and very very wrong — was already beginning to catch fire.

Morning came like a slap to the face.

Rajeev groaned, blindly smacking his phone alarm off the floor. His head felt like Simran's goldfish were holding a WWE match inside his skull.

Somewhere downstairs, he could hear Zayan and Meher arguing over who stole the last slice of cake.

Normal chaos. Comforting.

He blinked and open WhatsApp. Hundreds of notifications. Family group, college friends' group, colony group, one suspicious group called "Cool Dudes 2.0" that he didn't remember joining — all buzzing nonstop.

"Arre... why everyone so hyper in early morning yaar?" he muttered, scratching his head. Then he saw it.

Twitter. Trending.

@ProudRajeev95 — 48.9K likes | 10.7K retweets | 3.2K quote tweets

And the words staring back at him: "proper erection", "dicktaker ship"

Memes. Screenshots.

Even an edit where his face was photoshopped onto freedom fighter holding a bottle of Old Monk.

One meme showed him standing next to Political leader, looking confused under a caption that screamed:

"From midnight speeches to midnight tweets — Rajeev Bhaiya rewrites history, one typo at a time— Rajeev Bhaiya's English Revolution!"

Another one had his tweet printed on a fake newspaper:

"KANPUR MAN SOLVES INDIAN POLITICS IN 140 CHARACTERS".

Rajeev sat up straight so fast he almost blacked out. He scrolled desperately.

One journalist had even tagged India 24x365 News: "Sources: New political thinker emerging from the heartland! #RajeevBhaiyaForPM?"

His soul left his body for a second.

Downstairs, Aarushi was pouring herself black coffee like it was ammunition, fully ready to destroy anyone who talked too loud.

Her hair was in a lopsided bun that had clearly fought a battle with her pillow and lost. A few rogue strands framed her face, which was bare except for the faint trace of yesterday's kajal smudged under one eye — unintentionally perfect, like she belonged in a noir film about courtroom vengeance.

She wore an oversized T-shirt that said "I Object" in fading Helvetica, paired with pajama bottoms covered in tiny gavels. Even in half-woken chaos, she looked sharp — the kind of messy pretty that says: I haven't slept, I don't care, and I will still cross-examine your soul if you breathe wrong.

She heard Rajeev's horrified wail echo through the house:

"O Teri... MA KI TWEET!!!"

Simran looked up, concerned. "Bhaiya okay?" Aarushi raised one eyebrow. "Define okay." She opened her phone out of habit — and immediately saw it too. Rajeev's tweet.

The words.

The spelling.

The impact.

She closed her eyes. Counted to ten. Didn't help.

"This idiot," she whispered.

By now, Kabir and Rohan were reading the trending tweets aloud between snorts of laughter. "Listen, listen, someone wrote — 'This man didn't just break English; he buried it with full state honors.'"

"Arre yaar, poor Bhaiya," Simran said, torn between defending him and laughing herself. Meher high-fived Zayan.

"This is better than any show Netflix could make."

Rajeev stumbled down the stairs, looking like a man personally attacked by Wi-Fi.

"Aarushi ji," he gasped, "Bail please."

Aarushi didn't look up.

She sipped her coffee like a slow, deadly assassin and said, "Bail? From what? Your own vocabulary?"

Rajeev almost cried. "I didn't mean erection! I mean election! And dicktaker... was supposed to be dictator!"

He turned to the others, pleading.

"Explain them yaar. Emotion was pure!"

Zayan clapped him on the back, laughing.

"There was definitely emotion, bro. But your grammar? That needs to be rushed to the ICU."

Aarushi finally set her cup down and stood, crossing her arms.

"You realize you're a meme now, right? Half the country thinks you're either a freedom fighter or an adult film activist."

Rajeev looked ready to faint.

"Should I delete it? Erase the whole account like it never existed?"

Aarushi smirked. "Too late. Screenshots are forever."

She picked up her laptop and started typing furiously.

"What you can do is get ahead of this. Issue a clarification. Damage control before this turns into a court summons or worse."

"Summons?!" Rajeev squeaked like a cornered mouse.

"Relax," Aarushi said.

"But don't post anything without me checking it first."

Simran patted Rajeev's arm gently. "Bhaiya, at least you became famous?"

Meher cackled.

"Yeah. Just not for the reasons your parents prayed for."

Kabir adjusted his camera lens, grinning wickedly. "Smile, Rajeev Bhaiya. History is watching."

Rajeev flopped onto the sofa, face buried in a cushion. "It was just one innocent tweet" he mumbled mournfully.

"And I was caught up in the feeling of love..."

Aarushi paused. Their eyes found each other.

And in that breathless hush between moments, the world dimmed its roar— so even the trembling of heartbeats could be heard, soft as rain on distant glass.

She gave him a half-smile.

"Okay revolutionary. Let's clean up your mess."

Rajeev grinned back, his heart thudding in quiet rebellion.

Maybe—just maybe—every revolution began with a flicker of madness... and a whisper of love.

In the swirl of chaos, his only solace was time—time spent near Aarushi.

Time to watch the way stray strands of her hair danced onto her face, and how she brushed them away with a hint of irritation, a gesture so effortlessly human, it could make anyone fall in love without even knowing why.

CHAPTER 2

#VIRALBEFOREBREAKFAST

If there was a religion in India more powerful than cricket, more addictive than chai, and more eternal than marriage season…it was Breaking News.

And this morning, Rajeev Yadav was about to become its newest sacrificial goat.

At India 24x365 headquarters, the newsroom buzzed like a disturbed beehive.

Screens flashed "VIRAL TWEET FROM HEARTLAND MAN!" Hashtags screamed across the lower third:

🔺 #ProperErectionProtest 🔺 #DemocracyOrDicktaker 🔺 #RajeevRevolution 🔺

Inside the OB (Outside Broadcast) Van, Priyanka Sehgal applied her lipstick in the side mirror, barking into her mic "Gogi, shot ready? Need the lighting a bit dramatic… something with that 'gaon ka kranti-kaari' vibe."

Gogi, her eternally unimpressed cameraman, blew a bubble with his gum and adjusted the focus. "The drama meter's full, madam. Just make sure I get to lunch on time."

Priyanka laughed without humor.

"If this goes viral again, I will join some international news. Will take you with me... amm maybe"

"Just make sure I get free lunches there too" Gogi deadpanned.

The van screeched to a halt near the chai stall where the Chai Chronicles gang was currently hiding like oppressed freedom fighters.

Meanwhile, inside the tea stall ("their nerve centre") Rajeev was pacing like a trapped chicken. "I'll say my account was hacked!" he declared.

"You typed it drunk," Aarushi reminded, checking her notes.

"Hacking defense won't hold unless your liver or cyber cell can testify."

Simran was peeking nervously outside. "Bhaiya... they are here!" Meher casually leaned back, blowing smoke rings. "Let the circus begin."

Zayan was already practicing poses.

"If we go viral too, caption would be: 'Local hero, global impact.'"

Kabir clicked candids furiously, muttering, "This light is so poetic, man... humiliation against golden morning rays."

Rohan, the quiet stabilizer, sipped chai and whispered, "Rajeev, just apologize and move on. Don't think too much."

But it was too late.

Priyanka burst into the scene with the chaotic energy of a monsoon thunderstorm crashing into live prime time.

She wore a scarlet blazer far too loud for the hour, cinched dramatically at the waist like it was holding back national secrets. Her sunglasses were comically oversized — somewhere between film star and solar eclipse — and she didn't remove them indoors because, in her words, "Truth throws glare."

A laminated press badge bounced against her chest as she stormed forward, mic already in hand, its foam cover reading INDIA 24x365 like a warning label. She held it out not like a question, but a weapon — ready to jab quotes out of anyone who dared be silent.

Behind her, Gogi trudged in with the tripod slung over one shoulder and chewing gum like it owed him rent.

"Viewers, behold! This is the common man whose tweet shook the very foundations of politics!"

(She turned to Rajeev with theatrical flair)

Priyanka jabbed the mic closer, voice high on decibels and drama: "Sir! In your tweet, you mentioned a 'proper erection'! What message do you want to give to the nation?"

She didn't wait. Another jab.

"Are you implying the current government lacks... structural integrity?"

And before Rajeev could blink, the third one dropped like a headline grenade:

"Is this tweet part of a larger conspiracy, or was it just emotional intoxication? The nation deserves clarity! Is this the new normal— vulgar language, moral decay, and a cultural freefall playing out in real-time?"

Rajeev stared, frozen — like a student who studied the wrong syllabus for the viva of national dignity. His eyes darted between the mic, the camera lens, and Priyanka's too-intense sunglasses, which reflected his own panicked face back at him like a badly buffered meme.

He opened his mouth.

Nothing.

Not even a sound. Just the hollow echo of every English class he had skipped in Class 8. A bead of sweat betrayed him, rolling dramatically down his temple like it was trying to escape the scene.

Behind him, Aarushi audibly groaned. Kabir covered his face with the camera strap. Zayan whispered, "Don't say erection again, bhai... please."

Rajeev finally blinked. His lips moved, unsure whether they were about to form a word or a prayer. Just a dry cough that sounded suspiciously like a dying goat.

Gogi zoomed in mercilessly.

Rajeev blinked into the lens like a deer on Republic Day parade.

Aarushi stepped forward.

"Rajeev has no further comments right now. Any statement will be issued through proper channels."

Priyanka pounced. "Madam, why are you acting like a lawyer?"

"High Court," Aarushi said coolly.

"And currently functioning as his translator between English and common sense." The gang collectively tried not to laugh.

Priyanka sniffed, disappointed but calculating.

"Fine. But before you go, sir... a small message for your fans?"

Rajeev, panicking, blurted out the first thing that came to mind: "Don't be erection, be perfection!"

The world paused. Even the pigeons looked confused.

Aarushi covered her face with both hands. Kabir's camera shook with suppressed laughter.

Priyanka smiled like she had just won a Pulitzer. "Thank you, Rajeev ji," she said, victorious.

"And viewers, you heard it here first! A new philosophy is born!"

Gogi muttered under his breath, loud enough for only her: "Philosophy ya phillauri biscuit's advertisement?"

They packed up, leaving destruction in their wake.

At the same time, somewhere in a dingy party office, a junior political aide named Balli was glued to the TV, slurping chai from a cracked Superman mug.

As Rajeev's now-infamous "Don't be erection, be perfection" quote replayed for the fifth time, Balli paused, wiped his mouth, and muttered, "Sir ko yeh pasand aayega..."

He reached for his phone. "Potential asset spotted. Desi face. Viral reach. Full janta connect." Then he smirked. "Note this guy."

As the van roared away, Simran stared after them. "Bhaiya... now what?"

Rajeev sank into the plastic chair, shell-shocked. "nothing... just grave is needed to be dug"

Aarushi knelt down beside him, mock-serious.

"Listen, self-proclaimed internet freedom fighter," she said, her voice low but laced with fire, nudging his shoulder like a soldier waking another on the eve of battle.

"You haven't just tweeted a few clumsy words... You've declared war on the empire of English—and with reckless grace, you've slaughtered some of its finest warriors: grammar, clarity, and dignity," she said, a flicker of a smile dancing on her lips.

"You've done what rebels do—set fire without asking permission."

She paused.

Her eyes narrowed—not with ridicule, but with a strange, unspoken respect. The kind reserved for people too foolish to know fear... or too fearless to stay foolish.

"Just remember," she continued softly, "revolutions never arrive dressed for the part. They show up in typos, broken syntax, and the wrong choice of words. They begin not with perfection—but with the audacity to be imperfect in public."

She stepped back, letting the silence land. "History may laugh at you before it listens. But it does listen... eventually."

He looked at her, eyes heavy with quiet desperation.

"You're still with me... right?"

Their eyes met—closer now, breaths nearly touching.

And in that fragile pause, something warm moved between them— like a spark catching in the middle of a storm, beautiful... and far too dangerous.

Aarushi's gaze softened, lips curving with reluctant affection.

"I always stand by idiots," she whispered. "Just... don't make it a full-time job."

Rajeev smiled—wide, foolish, aching with gratitude.

Maybe—just maybe—this chaos, this madness, wasn't a collapse, but the beginning of something worth every broken rule.

Outside the chai stall, the crowd had doubled. Some were here for free chai, some for selfies, and some because something was trending — nobody knew exactly what.

It was giving full JCB ki khudai energy — a public spectacle where the content didn't matter, only the chaos did.

Rajeev, meanwhile, was sitting on the plastic stool like a dethroned prince, staring into nothingness.

Simran handed him a glass of water. "Bhaiya, it's okay na... just an accidental tweet..."

Rajeev looked at her blankly. " In an accident, it's usually the tyre that bursts... In my case, it felt like my whole life went flat."

Kabir, clicking a moody candid of Rajeev, muttered, "This... this is Pulitzer-winning sadness."

Just then, two new characters entered the frame:

A social media 'activist' uncle in kurta and a young meme page admin with pink hair.

Activist Uncle (adjusting his muffler): Rajeev ji, you are the new Gandhi of this new India!

This tweet... this isn't just a tweet—this is a revolution!

Meme Admin (typing rapidly): "Bro your face is now our new DP. #RajeevRoxx."

The two weren't random passersby—they were internet fixtures. Activist Uncle, famous for quoting the Constitution in every comment section, had already uploaded a selfie video starting with "See, beta..." and ending with "...and yet the mainstream media won't tell you this." His followers, mostly retired professors and rebel poets, flooded the replies with digital solidarity emojis.

Meanwhile, the pink-haired meme admin, known online as @DankSarkaar69, had just dropped a carousel titled "Rajeev's Guide to Accidental Uprisings", featuring GIFs, news clippings, and a clip of Rajeev scratching his nose in slow motion, captioned: "Democracy in action." It had been shared on 12,000 Instagram stories and counting.

Before Rajeev could respond, Priyanka from India 24x365 dramatically pointed her mic at him.

"Viewers, as you can see, democracy's new poster boy is here...Sir, when you posted that tweet, did you know you were about to start a revolution?

Rajeev, blinking rapidly, leaned into the mic. In a dead-serious tone, he said, "Madam, I was only searching for Wi-Fi... and somehow, I accidentally triggered the nation."

Gogi the cameraman SNORTED so loudly that even pigeons on the rooftop did a double-take.

The internet, meanwhile, was catching fire:

⊞ Trending Tweets:

> @SanskariSanskrit: "Respect to Rajeev Bhai. From Wedding Tent to Political Talent."

> @TandooriThanos: "If English is a weapon, Rajeev just fired a bazooka backwards."

> @Bhaktless: "New slogan: Rajeev Zindabad, Grammar Sharmsaar."

> @NewsWale: "BREAKING: Govt considering a 'Rajeev Act' to regulate drunk tweeting."

Meanwhile, Aarushi—arms crossed, jaw clenched—finally snapped.

"Enough. The circus is over. Rajeev, Be prepared. You are going to need a lawyer."

Rajeev, meek and hopeful, mumbled: "But... will I get one more chance to fix the spelling?"

Aarushi's glare could've turned iron to ash. And in that collective silence, everyone knew: Game over. Court case incoming.

Above them, the chai stall banner fluttered in the breeze, almost mocking — "Don't worry. Everything's fine."

In a dusty corner near the chai stall, where the paint had long given up on the walls and a rusty ceiling fan spun with more noise than breeze, Tau Hukum Singh leaned toward Chand Kaur. His weathered hands rested on his walking stick like bookmarks from another era.

He glanced at the crowd — all glued to their screens, recording, reposting, refreshing.

"Ek zamaana tha jab hum kitaabein padhte the" ("There was a time we studied books") he muttered, voice dry like parchment.

"Now... we study tweets."

Chand Kaur didn't look up from the small pile of gooseberries she was slicing for her next batch of homemade pickle.

"Aur retweet toh aise karte hain jaise Bhagavad Gita ke Shloka" ("And retweet them like they're gospel").

They sat in silence for a moment, two relics watching the theatre of modern outrage unfold. In the background, someone tried to chant a slogan but stumbled halfway through, distracted by a notification.

The sun climbed higher in the sky. Memes exploded across timelines. And Rajeev Yadav—ordinary, unsure, unforgettable—was officially crowned: The man who murdered English and accidentally woke up an entire nation.

And as the digital waves rippled far beyond the chai stall, India scrolled.

India laughed.

India raged.

And somewhere between a trending hashtag and a misspelled revolution, a mirror was quietly held up to a nation too busy performing to pause.

Rajeev Yadav, once just another face in the crowd, now stood unknowingly at the fault line between noise and meaning— mocked by many, misunderstood by most, but moved by something rare and quietly brave: the courage to speak, even when his words came out wrong.

Because sometimes, history doesn't begin with the right sentence— it begins with the wrong one, spoken out loud. In a country where truth is often curated, and silence dressed up as civility, maybe what we need isn't just perfect grammar— but imperfect honesty.

And if one foolish tweet can spark discomfort, laughter, outrage, and awakening— then maybe the revolution isn't coming.

Maybe it's already here.

And maybe... it begins with you.

CHAPTER 3

SUMMONS & FEELINGS

The FIR was filed at 8:17 AM.

By 8:19, someone -no one knows who – had already leaked a screenshot.

By 8:22, it was on three WhatsApp groups titled "Truth Shall Prevail ".

By 8:30, news anchors were speaking faster than usual, and hashtags had begun breeding like rabbits on heat.

Rajeev's sleepy town was now trending.

All because of 15 words, two typos, and a Wi-Fi signal that really shouldn't have worked.

The Complainant?

Advocate Teesta Rawat, National President of the Cyber Culture Protection Group — an NGO so committed to morality, it had once tried to ban emojis.

Her complaint, hand-delivered to the Rajnagar Police Station, read: "The accused has used vulgar, suggestive, and deeply anti-national language in public domain. The words 'erection' and 'dicktaker' are not only offensive, they are a direct attack on Indian democracy and Sanskriti."

The police, unsure whether to laugh or salute, did what they always did in such cases:

officially forwarded it to the cyber cell — and "unofficially" leaked it to the media again, just in case the first round had missed anyone.

By 10:17 AM, news tickers were screaming louder than the nation's conscience:

> ➤ KANPUR MAN UNDER LEGAL SCANNER FOR OBSCENE TWEET

> ➤ #RAJEEVROXX BUT LAW IS NOT LOLING

> ➤ NGO DEMANDS ARREST, CALLS IT "SOCIAL TERRORISM"

And at 10:40 AM sharp, just as Aarushi was finishing her second coffee and pretending to ignore the circus, her phone buzzed.

A message from her legal clerk: "Ma'am, an FIR's been filed. You're mentioned as possible counsel. Petitioner has moved for hearing. Date set. Judge Mishra. Be ready."

She blinked.

"Counsel?" she muttered aloud.

Then saw the attachment — a press clipping from India24x365:

"Sources say Rajeev Yadav may be defended by his 'close associate and reputed lawyer' Aarushi Malhotra."

She didn't know what stunned her more:

> ➤ The word "close associate,"

> ➤ The word "reputed,"

> ➤ Or the fact that her picture had been used without permission — and filtered badly.

Aarushi's heels struck the pavement like closing arguments — fast, final, unforgiving. But even as she advanced, a stray memory slipped through: her ex, Mr. MBA-with-perfect-English, who once called her "overly reactive" and sent a breakup email with bullet points. Fluent in grammar. Bankrupt in honesty.

Since then, she'd stopped trusting fluency. Real truth didn't wear polish. It stumbled, stammered — like Rajeev.

And then, in slow-motion worthy of a Bollywood climax, Aarushi Malhotra marched across the scene. Long kurta flaring slightly with each step, black shades pulled down just enough to reveal eyes sharp enough to file a lawsuit, Aarushi wasn't walking — she was issuing summons with her presence.

The air around the chai stall had turned sticky — a heady mix of dust, chai fumes, and rising panic. Aarushi slowly scanned the area, shoulders stiff with rage.

She found Rajeev on a faded wooden bench with one wobbly leg, mid-gesture, looking far too pleased with himself for someone trending on national television. He was busy giving an interview to a YouTuber titled "Desi Digital Dangal".

"Zayan, get him off camera."

"Why? He's talking about freedom of—"

"—He's about to lose the freedom to breathe."

She marched forward and tapped Rajeev hard on the head with a rolled-up newspaper.

"Congratulations," she said flatly. "You've gone from trending topic to legal liability."

Rajeev blinked. "Wait... someone actually filed a case?"

"Yes," she snapped. "You've been accused of public obscenity, promoting enmity, and linguistic genocide."

"Genocide?!"

"That one's unofficial. That's just me speaking as a citizen."

She took a deep breath. "We're going to court."

Rajeev, still clutching his cracked phone like a holy relic, whispered to Simran, "Looks like the hunt for bail has officially begun..."

Then, after a pause, softer — as if confessing to the air more than to her —"And maybe... the lawyer I'm falling for is the one holding the map."

Simran squeaked. "Bhaiya, seeing Di's mood... I'm getting flashbacks of my kindergarten principal!"

Ignoring the commotion, Aarushi stood in front of Rajeev and crossed her arms — the universal posture for "I'm about to ruin your life and save it at the same time."

She spoke slowly, like a lawyer explaining the terms of parole.

"Rajeev. You're trending. You're famous. You have a legal case to defend."

Rajeev blinked.

"Famous... you mean, like, I could get a call from The Kapil Sharma Show?"

Aarushi removed her shades. "More like Tihar Jail."

She leaned in, voice low but firm.

"This isn't just online tamasha, Rajeev. If this FIR escalates under IPC 505 or IT Act Section 67, you're looking at more than embarrassment. Think censorship. Travel bans. Even losing your voting rights if they frame it as promoting enmity."

She paused, her eyes narrowing.

"Do you really want to be the first man in Indian history disqualified from democracy because of autocorrect?"

Rajeev blinked, visibly deflating.

Zayan, trying to lighten the mood, piped up: "Di, they do have ACs in jail for high-profile people, right?"

Aarushi gave him a death stare so intense that Zayan physically took two steps back and pretended to check his phone.

Kabir, meanwhile, was already writing a poetic caption in his head "In the court of public opinion, even clowns need a lawyer..."

"LISTEN UP," Aarushi barked, snapping them all back to reality.

She pointed at Rajeev. "You're not allowed to talk to the media. No tweets, no posts, no forwarded good mornings on WhatsApp. NOTHING."

Rajeev nodded frantically like an intern in front of an angry boss. Next, she pointed at the group. "You idiots — no Insta lives, no reels, no commentary. This is not your vlog material. This is a legal landmine."

Meher, arms folded, smirked. "Not even one meme, Di?"

Aarushi turned to her, deadpan.

"One meme. And you'll be tattooing 'Contempt of Court' on your forehead."

Simran giggled nervously. Meher saluted dramatically.

Aarushi pulled out her phone, dialing rapidly to her intern.

"Hello? ...Yes, Aarushi here. Listen — I need urgent anticipatory bail paperwork started. No, not for me. My—"

(She glanced at Rajeev, then pinched the bridge of her nose.)

"—our emotionally unstable client."

On the other end, law intern and part-time caffeine addict Riva, was already fumbling with papers and speaking too fast:

"Yes ma'am! Of course! Bail! Section... something... I'll open Bare Act PDF now—just give me two minutes and maybe... a charger."

Aarushi closed her eyes. She'd known war zones with more composure.

Meanwhile, not far away, Priyanka Sehgal was standing in front of her news van, now LIVE on India 24x365.

"Viewers, the nation demands answers! Was this tweet a drunken mistake or a calculated act of rebellion? Reporting live from ground zero, where chai is free but grammar costs lives—"

Behind her, Gogi zoomed in on Rajeev's confused face, adding sarcastically under his breath,

"National hero or national headache — let public decide..."

As Aarushi clicked her phone shut, she glanced around at the chaos unfurling like a badly scripted reality show.

Street kids darted past with handmade posters screaming #RajeevRocks. A group of aunties huddled over their smartphones, debating fiercely on WhatsApp whether Rajeev was a freedom fighter, a cultural offender dragging down Bhartiya Sanskriti or just another youth lost to bad English.

And across the road, a momo stall had hung a banner: "Democracy Discount — 10% Off If You Say Jai Hindi!"

She exhaled slowly. This wasn't just a PR nightmare. It was a cultural trainwreck. And it was happening on live television.

She turned back to Rajeev, softer now. "Listen, Rajeev..."

Her voice dropped low, almost kind.

"You're a good guy. But the world doesn't care about that. They care about... image. Narrative. English."

Rajeev looked genuinely hurt for a second. Then he scratched his head and said, "But tell me... the grammar of the heart — that's still flawless, isn't it?"

Aarushi's tough exterior cracked for a fraction of a second — a tiny smile tugged at the corner of her mouth.

He hesitated, then added quietly, eyes not leaving hers: "And... as my lawyer... do you believe I can still come out of this clean?"

It was an innocent enough question — phrased like legal reassurance.

But something in the way he said believe lingered in the air, soft and unmissable.

Aarushi met his gaze.

As his lawyer, she should've answered immediately. As herself... she wasn't sure she could.

She shook her head and muttered, "crazy boy..."

And just like that, she grabbed his wrist and pulled him away from the chaos — no words, no warning, just the kind of grip that said: move now, explain later.

(Rajeev felt as if the Lord Himself had bound him to the finest of His creations with a thread no eye could see but every soul could feel. In that fleeting moment, he surrendered—utterly and without resistance— his soul to her, be she his love, his counsel, or simply the silence that understood him.)

"..No more democracy talk. No more erection mistakes. Come on. We need to save your sorry ass."

Rajeev stumbled after her, yelling over his shoulder at the gang: "Guys! If I end up behind bars... you all better take care of my Twitter password!

The gang saluted, laughing and hooting, as Aarushi dragged the nation's newest internet accident toward legal redemption.

Outside Rajnagar Nyayalaya, the air smelled of aging paper, sweaty tension, and burnt samosas.

The building itself looked like it had once aspired to grandeur but settled somewhere between bureaucratic fatigue and mild neglect — pale yellow walls streaked with paan stains, a creaky fan on every balcony and just inside the lobby, a dusty portrait of Gandhi stared down from the wall — glass cracked, frame crooked, yet somehow still watching like a witness who never left the courtroom.

Aarushi was striding toward the lawyer's block when she suddenly stopped near a rusty tea cart under a neem tree.

She dropped Rajeev's wrist.

"Wait," she said, pinching the bridge of her nose.

It was a habit Rajeev had always found strangely endearing — like her brain needed a second to reload before delivering a verdict.

But right now, even that familiar gesture tightened something in his chest. If Aarushi was pausing, it meant things were worse than he thought.

Rajeev blinked. What happened? My bail won't get cancelled... right?

Aarushi didn't reply right away. Instead, she turned to the tea seller and said softly, "One strong chai, please. Extra ginger. No cardamom — he never gets it right."

Rajeev followed, just a step behind, his voice barely above a whisper.

"Can you make one for me too... maybe with a little less stress stirred in?"

Their hands brushed as they reached for the cups. Neither pulled away. The steam rose lazily between them, like a white flag in a battlefield.

Aarushi finally spoke, low and tired. "You know, Rajeev... sometimes I envy you."

Rajeev almost dropped his kulhad.

"Me? Envy? My english speaking skills?"

She gave a dry laugh. "No, donkey. Your heart." Rajeev frowned, genuinely confused.

"My heart? That anyway belongs to you!"

Aarushi chuckled despite herself — that rare, musical laugh that even courtrooms couldn't summon from her.

She stirred her chai absent-mindedly.

"You... say what you feel. Even when you crash grammar into a truck and set it on fire, you're real," she said softly. "In my world — in court, in politics, in media — everyone speaks perfect English but means nothing."

Rajeev stared at her, stunned. For once, he didn't try to crack a joke. Instead, he said — shyly, honestly: You know... when I look into your eyes... I see the truth. The words were clumsy. The moment wasn't. For a second, neither of them said anything.

The courtroom inside pulsed with restless energy — murmurs rising like static, clerks shouting names that echoed off peeling walls, the clatter of heels and the shuffle of papers merging into a chaotic symphony.

Lawyers in black robes moved like shadows sharpening at the edges — collars tugged high like ceremonial armor, their silence tight with tension.

Eyes scanned the room like searchlights over enemy terrain, and in their throats, arguments coiled like vipers—quiet, waiting, deadly.

But for Rajeev, it all blurred — a distant, distorted murmur, like a radio stuck between stations. His heart was pounding too loudly to hear anything else.

The judge's bench loomed above, indifferent yet monumental. The smell of old wood and fresh ink mixed with the sweat of worry. Every breath felt borrowed. Every second stretched.

And in that sea of legal jargon and procedural noise, Rajeev sat still — a misfit in a theatre of law, clutching silence like it was the only truth he had left. In that moment, it seemed as if there were only two people in the world — Rajeev and Aarushi, accidentally colliding in the mess of ambition, fear, and unexpected affection.

Then Aarushi smirked and quietly went back to flipping through the documents, as if none of it had touched her at all.

"That's enough. Emotion time's over. Let's go — we have an anticipatory bail to file."

Rajeev saluted dramatically, throwing imaginary stars around himself.

"Yes Milord... I am emotional content pending!"

Aarushi shook her head, laughing under her breath as they headed inside.

And in that small, chaotic corner of Delhi's forgotten court system, a tiny, stubborn love story had just found its first breath.

It wasn't perfect. But then again — neither were they. And maybe that's why it would survive.

Not far away — in a dimly lit party office above a mattress showroom in Gurugram, Vikas Tyagi leaned back in his faux-leather chair, eyes scanning the TV screen where Rajeev's courtroom clip was playing on loop.

He sipped his black coffee with the smugness of a man watching someone else's blunder become his golden opportunity.

"This idiot..." he murmured, "is exactly what we need."

His assistant, Rehan looked up from his laptop. "Sir, he's trending in Tier 2 and Tier 3 audiences. Desi gold. Emotional connect. Illiterate but lovable. Full mass appeal."

Vikas smiled like a man who had just found a lottery ticket in a dustbin.

"Start working on Phase One," he said calmly. "We'll make Rajeev Yadav the reluctant voice of the people. Aam aadmi meets accidental icon."

"Sir, what if he refuses?"

"Then we say he's neutral. And in Indian politics, neutrality means you're already with the opposition."

CHAPTER 4

MILORDNESS, HAVE MERCY

In Courtroom No. 2 of the Rajnagar Nyayalaya, the ceiling fans turned with the lazy determination of bored buffaloes in peak summer — slow, heavy, and utterly unimpressed by justice.

A dusty board read: "Satyamev Jayate." (Truth Alone Triumphs)

Bold. Timeless. Sacred.

But someone — some mischievous mind with a ballpoint pen and too much free time — had scribbled beneath it:

'Terms and Conditions Apply.'

Rajeev thought, Huh... Truth alone triumphs — but only after it clears background checks, political filters, and public opinion polls.

The chaos was noticeable now— slowly brewing in raised voices, restless feet, and the growing rustle of paperwork. Advocates shuffled in like black-coated penguins. The audience benches groaned under the weight of gossip-hungry onlookers, journalists scribbled furiously, and somewhere in the far corner of the court, Gogi the cameraman was adjusting his tripod —angling for the first visual like it was breaking news and not just broken protocol.

In the center, standing awkwardly beside Aarushi, was Rajeev. In a borrowed blazer. Three sizes too big.

He whispered, "Is there no AC in here? I'm sweating like a politician in a lie detector test."

Aarushi elbowed him sharply just as Hon'ble Justice (Retd.) V.P. Mishra entered — spectacles balanced delicately on his nose, a file of handwritten notes tucked under one arm, and, quite curiously, a thin paperback of Bollywood Shayari under the other.

Though officially retired, Justice Mishra had been called back on extended service — a special appointment for high-sensitivity matters that apparently required both legal wisdom and a flair for poetic dramatics.

The bailiff, Manoj Bhaiya, bellowed: "Court is now in season... I mean, session!"

The hall half-heartedly rose.

A lawyer's phone blared "Pani Pani" ringtone before being hastily silenced.

Justice Mishra settled into his chair with a grunt, scanned the file, and muttered, Twitter tweet viral... democracy erection... dictatorkarship... what absolute nonsense is this? Ab ye sab dekhne ke liye retirement se vaapis bulaya gaya hai? (And I've been pulled out of retirement to deal with this circus?)

He looked up, fixing his piercing, heavily-spectacled stare on Rajeev. "You are... Mr. Rajiv Yadav?"

Rajeev stood bolt upright. "Yes, Sir Your Milordness!"

Aarushi facepalmed hard enough to rattle her own glasses.

Judge Mishra massaged his forehead, as if physically squeezing patience into his brain. "Advocate Aarushi Malhotra, kindly... elucidate the matter in brief."

Aarushi stepped forward, crisp and composed. "Milord, the petitioner alleges that my client posted a politically sensitive tweet due to which —"

Before she could finish, Advocate Teesta Rawat (opposing counsel, media darling) rose dramatically like a Bollywood villainess entering second half.

"Milord, objection!" Advocate Rawat thundered, raising her hand as if delivering the final line in a courtroom thriller.

"This is not just a tweet — it is a gravitational offense! It has disrupted the socio-constitutional equilibrium of this great nation! Democracy itself is wobbling, Your Lordship!"

Justice Mishra blinked. Slowly.

He adjusted his spectacles with exaggerated calm, then said, deadpan: "Advocate Rawat... what, in the name of common sense, is a gravitational offense?"

Teesta flushed but covered quickly:

"Milord, I meant... grave offense. Gravity, grave... you know... same orbit, Milord!"

From the audience, someone snorted. It was probably one of the unpaid law interns, for whom moments like this made it all just about worth it.

Mishra sighed the sigh of a man who knew he was not paid enough for this. Turning to Aarushi, he asked, "What exactly did your client tweet?"

Aarushi cleared her throat and read from the printout. "Milord, the exact words were:

"This country needs a proper erection, not this dicktaker ship. Jai Hindi."

A pin-drop silence fell.

The courtroom froze.

The fans didn't just pause — they hiccupped.

Somewhere, a file slipped from a clerk's hand and landed like a gavel of disbelief.

Even Justice Mishra stopped mid-page turn — his spectacles sliding halfway down his nose as if trying to escape the moment.

A few benches creaked under the weight of held-in laughter. One junior lawyer choked on his own breath.

Rajeev, sensing the growing awkwardness, scrambled to explain himself:

"Milordness, I thought 'erection' was like... the bigger version of 'election'. You know, double powerful!"

Justice Mishra froze. Then, with the calm despair of a man questioning his career choices, he shut the case file with a loud thwack.

"This isn't a matter for the IPC," he muttered, rubbing his temples.

"This is a first-degree murder of the English language."

He cleared his throat and turned poetic, eyes distant, voice heavy with misplaced gravitas:

"When words are used without thought or care, Even truth starts gasping for air."

Silence. Utter silence.

Nobody understood what it meant.

Not the clerk. Not the lawyers.

Not even Justice Mishra himself.

But the delivery? Oscar-worthy.

But it sounded weighty enough that Manoj Bhaiya nodded solemnly and Pinky, the court clerk, started secretly live-tweeting from her phone.

⊞ @CourtroomConfessions: "BREAKING: Accused just said 'Milordness'. Legal system now requesting therapy. #RajeevRevolution"

Meanwhile, outside, India 24x365 had already flashed the headline: BREAKING: Local Man Arrested for "Erection Tweet"? Twitter Divided!

In the corner of the courtroom, Vikas Tyagi's party interns had started trending #RajeevForReform while also simultaneously trolling him with memes like:

➢ "Baba Rajeev's English Speaking Classes: Enrollment Open"

➢ "New symbol of free erection... I mean, election."

In the middle of all this, Rajeev leaned towards Aarushi and whispered:

"I'm not sure if I'm having a panic attack or just need samosas," Rajeev whispered.

Aarushi didn't look at him. "Both. But we'll survive court first. Hold it. We're making history here."

Judge Mishra, now visibly tired of his own existence, rubbed his temples like he was regretting every career decision since law school. He looked at Rajeev, sighed deeply, and said:

"This is not sedition. This is not obscenity. This is... unfortunate spelling."

Judge Mishra banged his gavel gently, like even the gavel was too tired for drama.

"Court grants anticipatory bail. The accused is advised to refrain from tweeting without adult supervision. Also, stop blaming autocorrect — it has suffered enough."

He turned to the prosecution.

"And the Police is directed not to arrest him unless he attempts to trend another revolution."

Rajeev beamed like he'd just won a Padma Shri.

Aarushi grabbed his sleeve before he could say anything foolish and started leading him out.

But before she reached the door, she turned back sharply.

"Milord, we would also like to move for quashing of the FIR — this entire matter lacks merit and reeks of political misuse."

Judge Mishra gave her a long stare — part respect, part exhaustion.

"Fine. File your application. I'll list it after fifteen days."

He muttered to himself as he scribbled on his notes, "God save this country... from grammar and grandstanding."

The courtroom buzzed, memes flew, and somewhere, in a corner of Twitter, the legend of Rajeev Bhaiya — India's accidental rebel — was just beginning.

Outside the heavy iron gates of Rajnagar Nyayalaya, the real courtroom had shifted to the streets. Media vans lined the dusty road like battle tanks. Microphones jabbed in every direction.

Chaiwalas were selling "Breaking News Chai" and hawkers had even started selling "I 🩶 Erection" badges just for the memes. It was as if the country had suddenly discovered a progressive mindset, one that didn't flinch at big taboos or small spelling errors — as long as it could laugh, share, and trend.

Gogi leaned on his van door, munching a samosa, watching the frenzy like a disinterested god. Priyanka Sehgal was already in full-on TV mode, talking into her mic with the speed of a Mumbai local.

"Viewers, behold! Rajeev Yadav — a common citizen — has now become the epicenter of a national debate, all because of a single viral tweet. It seems... even the word 'erection' now demands serious discussion in this country!"

Somewhere behind her, Balli, the part-time speech repeater, of Vikas Tyagi's political party was trying to start a random chant:

"All hail Rajeev Bhaiya! The right to errr..election is our fundamental right!"

Nobody understood what he meant. Including Balli.

Meanwhile, the gang had huddled together under an old banyan tree inside the court premises. Kabir clicked a photo of Rajeev looking miserable and captioned it on Instagram:

"Sometimes the revolution you start is not the revolution you meant. #ErectionSensation #RajeevBhaiya"

Meher was laughing so hard she had to sit down.

"Bro, you seriously need to launch your own brand now — 'Rajeev's Wrong English Tuition Classes'!" she giggled, lighting a beedi.

Zayan chimed in with a grin, "And the slogan will be: 'Speak like a legend, fail like a pro!'"

Even Simran, the eternal sunshine girl, had tears of laughter in her eyes. "Bhaiya, don't worry! The bigger the name, the dumber the mistake. It's practically tradition.!" she chirped, handing him a cupcake she had randomly baked for "stress relief."

Rajeev, now half-dead from embarrassment and half-alive from sugar rush, looked at Aarushi, who was furiously typing something on her phone.

"Everyone's just making fun of me..." he said, his voice barely holding together, cracking at the edges.

Aarushi looked up, the teasing gone from her eyes — replaced by something quieter. Something that listened.

For a second, all the noise, all the mocking, all the memes — faded.

She saw not the clown, not the trending hashtag — but Rajeev. Her Rajeev. The boy who loved too honestly, who spoke too clumsily, who fought with the world in broken English but a full heart.

She tucked her phone away and walked up to him. In front of everyone, she grabbed Rajeev's hand. Firmly. Like a lawyer closing her best argument.

"Listen up, everyone," she said, her voice cutting through the madness.

"Laugh all you want. Meme all you want. But when the dust settles, remember — it's easy to joke. It's harder to stand up and own your mistakes. Rajeev is standing. That's more than most of you ever do."

A silence fell.

Even Meher put out her beedi. Kabir lowered his camera. Simran sniffled and whispered, "Wow Di..."

Zayan fake-clapped and muttered, "Ok, lawyer flex. Respect."

Rajeev looked at Aarushi like she had just punched the whole world in the face for him.

And secretly, somewhere deep in his bindaas Kanpuriya heart, a small dhol started beating: Dhaak... dhaak... dhaak...

In that moment, Rajeev realized something. This wasn't just about F.I.R. anymore. It was about who would fight for you when even your own words turned against you. And Aarushi Malhotra had just fought for him.

Maybe, just maybe... she was the real revolution he needed.

Because sometimes, love doesn't raise a flag — it stands silently beside you while the world tries to tear you down.

Across the tea stalls, panchayats, and air-conditioned offices of Delhi NCR, one thing united everyone: Everyone had an opinion on Rajeev Yadav.

And Rajeev?

He was sitting at the same chai tapri with Kabir, Meher, Zayan, Simran, Rohan and Arushi, dunking a Parle- G into cutting chai, looking very, very confused.

"I still don't understand... how someone like me ended up being called a hero." he said, genuinely.

Kabir clicked a photo of Rajeev's innocent face under the flickering bulb and whispered,

"Because sometimes, bro... the world needs a fool to show its own foolishness."

And somewhere, behind all the noise, something inside Aarushi stirred — an odd mix of fondness and fear.

Maybe it wasn't just Rajeev who had gone viral. Maybe they all were about to.

CHAPTER 5

LOVE IN THE TIME OF TYPO

Aarushi Malhotra had fought real battles before. Custody cases that tore families apart. Land disputes uglier than soap operas. Corporate suits where smiles hid daggers.

But nothing had prepared her for this —

Defending a man who wasn't even hers, yet somehow felt like her responsibility. A man whose crime was murdering English at 2 A.M.

She sat in her tiny office above a perpetually humming photocopy shop, papers scattered around like a battlefield. On one side:

- ➢ Screenshots of Rajeev's "Erection Tweet."

- ➢ Memes comparing Rajeev to Shakespeare's drunk cousin.

- ➢ A Court Notice

- ➢ Her own notes in rapid handwriting:

On the other side:

- ➢ Her own notes in rapid handwriting:

    "Misuse of IPC 505 (2) — attempt to spread public alarm without actual incitement." "Intent matters. Mistake ≠ Malice."

    "Highlight cultural obsession with English — social satire, not sedition."

"No mens rea. No public harm. Just public humour."

"Constitutional right to be wrong — Article 19(1)(a)."

"Remind: Even Supreme Court said jokes ≠ seditious."

"Context. Tone. Satire. All missing from FIR."

She slammed her pen down. "So now, in this country, even a spelling mistake qualifies as sedition?" she said under her breath.

From the corner of the office, Riva looked up, blinking like a raccoon caught in harsh fluorescent light. Mug in one hand, highlighter in the other, she was surrounded by legal printouts, two charging cables, and what appeared to be the cold remains of her third coffee.

"Okay but like... what if he meant erection metaphorically?"

Aarushi stared at her. "Riva."

"I'm just saying. Maybe it was, like, performance art? A protest tweet disguised as bad grammar?"

"Riva."

Riva immediately scribbled something in her notebook and muttered, "Sorry. Continuing research. Please ignore me."

Meanwhile, on the sofa, Rajeev sat like a schoolboy awaiting results, nervously fiddling with a Rubik's cube Simran had given him for "focus therapy."

"Aarushi..." he said softly, "tell me I'm not headed to jail for a tweet..."

Aarushi looked at him — genuinely looked. The creases of worry on his forehead. The way his legs kept jittering uncontrollably. The shame under his typical 'confident clown' smile. For a second, she forgot the case, the chaos, the circus outside. She only saw Rajeev. Raw. Afraid. Real.

"You don't belong in jail," she said, voice steady.

"You belong in chaos, in confusion... maybe even in a few textbooks on stupidity — but never in a courtroom for crimes."

Rajeev blinked, unsure if it was a compliment or a roast. (It was both.)

Aarushi stood up, pacing. "See Rajeev. In cases like these, Courtrooms are not about truth. They're about narratives. Storytelling. Evidence. Drama."

She pointed at him, eyes sharp.

"What's your story, huh? Clueless clown? Political pawn? Or an accidental freedom fighter?"

Rajeev scratched his head, sheepish.

"All I ever wanted was to be the Shahrukh of the streets... Now look at me — I've turned into a national-level idiot."

Aarushi's lips twitched. And for the first time since this entire circus began, she smiled — a real, tired, beautifully affectionate smile.

"Idiot or Shahrukh... doesn't matter. You're my client now. And I don't quit. I fight. And I win. Got it, Mr. ProudRajeev95?

Rajeev stared at her, mesmerized. Not because of her words. But because of the fire in her eyes — The kind that made lost people believe in happy endings again.

He didn't know if he would win the case. But he knew he had already won something bigger. Aarushi Malhotra's faith.

And maybe... just maybe... Her heart too.

By noon, Aarushi had switched gears completely. Gone was the Aarushi who teased and smiled and threatened to disown Rajeev for his grammar crimes.

Now?

Now she was Advocate Aarushi Malhotra, black blazer sharp as her arguments, hair tied back into a no-nonsense bun, legal notes color-coded and ready to kill.

Rajeev sat in the corner, still twiddling with the Rubik's cube, still looking like a man about to be sacrificed to democracy.

"Let's rehearse," Aarushi said briskly, pacing like a general before war.

"If the judge asks you what your intent was behind the tweet, how would you defend?"

Rajeev straightened up like a guilty toddler.

"Milord, all I wanted was for the country to have an erection—"

"No, no, no!" Aarushi nearly screamed, hurling a cushion at his head.

"It's election, Rajeev! Election! Are you trying to get me arrested too?"

Rajeev ducked just in time, laughing nervously.

"Milord, my intent was to say — we need fair elections, not dictatorship. Just a little... English malfunction, that's all."

Aarushi pinched the bridge of her nose but stopped when she felt Rajeev's eyes on her, soft and searching in a way that made her unexpectedly shy.

Better. But slower," Aarushi coached, narrowing her eyes.

"And look at the judge with those innocent eyes — like you're the world's sweetest, most harmless little goat being sent to slaughter."

Rajeev tried making a 'sad puppy' face. It looked... disturbing.

Aarushi sighed, but inside, she was melting a little.

This idiot — this absolute adorable idiot — was actually trusting her with his whole future.

There was a knock.

Kabir and Meher barged in, carrying chai and a brown packet.

"We got him a new shirt just for court," Meher announced proudly, tossing a packet at Rajeev.

"Baby pink — to soften the judge's mood a little."

"And I brought some motivational dialogues" Kabir added, handing Aarushi a crumpled piece of paper.

"Just in case he needs to sound like a tragic hero instead of a Twitter accident. Like 'Freedom of speech is fundamental!' or 'Error is human!' Got it?"

Rohan, lounging against the desk with his arms crossed, smirked.

"You should've just bought a book of Bollywood shayari. At least then the judge might cry and grant relief."

Aarushi shook her head at their chaos — but she was smiling. Their madness was her strength now.

As Rajeev tried on the new shirt (inside-out, obviously), Aarushi caught herself staring. Not at his clothes. Not at his clumsy panic.

But at him — the man who could have easily hidden, deleted, denied. And yet he stood here — flawed, frightened, foolish — but honest.

Somewhere deep inside, a voice whispered: "This is the kind of man you fight for."

Not the perfect ones. Not the polished ones. The real ones.

Outside, the media vans were already gathering. Microphones, cameras, hashtags waiting like vultures.

Inside, Aarushi picked up her file, adjusted her black coat, and smiled grimly.

"Ready to trend for the right reasons this time, Mr. ProudRajeev95?" Rajeev gave a shaky thumb-up.

"Just one request..." he said, his voice trembling ever so slightly.

"If they allow Maggi in jail... could you send me a packet, Aarushi?"

Aarushi laughed — a full, fearless sound that echoed like truth through the narrow chambers of their cluttered office.

In that moment, for Rajeev Yadav, the courtroom faded into irrelevance. The memes? Overruled. The nation's noise? Struck off the record.

All that remained on the bench of his heart was that laugh — pure, unscripted, and admissible as hope. And the woman who, despite the evidence, still believed he was worth defending.

The afternoon sun dipped low, casting a tired golden light into Aarushi's office. The clock ticked too loudly. The weight of tomorrow pressed heavy on everyone's shoulders.

The group had gone silent after the brief rehearsal chaos.

Simran had curled up on the couch, scrolling through inspirational quotes on Pinterest. Rohan sat hunched over his laptop in the corner, headphones in, tabs open. One showed a sleek landing page titled "ProudRajeev95: Voice of the Streets" in bold red. Another was a drafted blog post with the headline: "Accidental Icon. Intentional Impact."

He wasn't doing it for credit. He just couldn't watch the internet eat someone alive without offering a backup plan.

"You're coding again?" Simran asked, peeking.

"Crisis kit," Rohan replied flatly. "Media primer. Website. A few scripted one-liners if he forgets how to talk."

"God, I love how you say 'one-liners' like you're designing Iron Man."

Kabir and Meher, unfazed, were now whisper-fighting over the right playlist for Rajeev's "pre-court motivation session." (Meher insisted on Eminem. Kabir voted for Lucky Ali.)

And Rajeev? Rajeev was staring at Aarushi like she was the only anchor keeping him from drowning.

Aarushi noticed. She always noticed.

"What's this, hmm? Starting a new trend — flirting through eye contact only?" she teased, sauntering over with two cutting chai glasses.

Rajeev took the chai carefully, still gazing at her like she was some sacred thing.

"You're like... oxygen," he said suddenly, voice soft but certain. "Whenever I panic... I just look at you. And I can breathe again."

Aarushi froze for a second. Not because of the words. Because of how genuinely unpolished they were.

There was no smoothness. No attempt to impress. Just pure, terrifying, unfiltered truth.

She softened for a second... then masked it with a smirk.

"Wow. Planning to kill me with metaphors now? Oxygen? Really? Couldn't come up with anything less dramatic?"

"No, I mean it," Rajeev said, earnest, clumsy — and somehow, heartbreakingly honest. "I'm not scared of you. I'm scared of the world. But when you're around... everything feels just a little easier."

Aarushi stared at him, her legal mind racing to find loopholes, defenses, distractions — anything to avoid what she was feeling.

But there was none. Rajeev wasn't arguing a case. He wasn't pleading. He was just being.

And maybe that's what Aarushi had been craving all along. Not someone perfect. Someone present.

Without thinking, she reached out and straightened the crooked collar of his new shirt. Tiny act. Massive earthquake inside both of them.

"You're not doing this for the court... right?" Rajeev whispered. "You're doing it for me... aren't you?"

Aarushi arched an eyebrow. "Don't push your luck, Mr. Erection Tweet."

But her fingers lingered a second longer than necessary. And Rajeev's smile grew — that reckless, heart-first, Kanpuriya smile.

They stood like that, two stubborn idiots in denial, pretending the world outside hadn't already exploded.

Only when Simran giggled from the couch did Aarushi snap out of it.

"Alright, alright — cut the hero-heroine poses now," Simran called out, lobbing a cushion at them. "You've got courtroom prep, not a wedding shoot!"

Everyone burst out laughing. Even Aarushi. Even Rajeev.

And for a few fleeting minutes, they all forgot the hashtags, the cameras, the mockery. They were just friends. Fighting life together. One bad joke, one mistake, one chai at a time.

CHAPTER 6

BREAKING NEWS, BROKEN ENGLISH

Somewhere in the cluttered newsroom of India 24x365 — 11:45 PM

"It's all about TRPs, Priyanka. Either ride the wave — or get left behind."

The editor barked over the newsroom din, waving his half-eaten vada pav like a conductor's baton at a very confused orchestra.

Priyanka Sehgal didn't flinch. She was already editing her next headline in her head:

"Viral Villain or Voice of Democracy? The Rajeev Yadav Phenomenon!"

On the giant screen behind her, Rajeev's drunken tweet — "proper erection not dicktaker ship" — blinked like a neon crime scene. It was blurred for "decency," but in a way that somehow made it look even more scandalous. Someone from the media team had helpfully added a "breaking news" siren effect — just in case the scandal needed extra masala.

Priyanka's lips curled into a smirk. She loved days like this. Low effort. High drama. Endless prime-time shouting.

"Gogi!" she barked, snapping her fingers.

Gogi adjusted his indoor sunglasses and sauntered over, chewing his gum like he had all the time in the world.

"What now, madam — planning to shoot a film inside the courtroom?"

"No" Priyanka said, eyes gleaming with purpose.

"Court comes later. First, we build the drama — emotional montage, sad violin music, slow zoom on Rajeev Bhaiya's innocent face...We're going to squeeze every last drop of TRP out of this."

"And when do we get lunch?" Gogi asked, deadpan.

"Lunch?" Priyanka scoffed like a war general. "Not until Twitter starts sharing our clip. Until then — we starve for the nation."

Gogi sighed, popping another gum into his mouth. "In this country, controversy feeds faster than food."

Without missing a beat, Priyanka leaned toward the producer's desk.

"Ankit! Get the graphics ready — headline: 'The Rise of Rajeev: The New Voice of the Nation?'

She raised an eyebrow and smirked ever so slightly, "I'll make sure to... emphasise the rise. And make the font sparkle a bit. It's for youth engagement."

In the background, the 'serious' news team — who were supposed to be covering a drought report — watched with amused detachment, sipping lukewarm machine coffee, as their newsroom gracefully descended into a full-blown meme factory.

Cut to: Live Panel Promo Flashing On Screens

◌ *"Tonight 9 PM:

> ➤ Is Rajeev Yadav the accidental freedom fighter India needs?

> ➤ Err..ection vs Election: Language, Leadership, and Laughter!

> ➤ Special guest: Meme Creator @SharmaJi_Ne_Bola."*

Hashtags had already started trending: #RajeevRevolution

#ErectionError #DemocracyKaDharohar

Meanwhile, just outside Simran's house, the gang was getting a taste of fame — the wrong kind. A reporter from a local tabloid had somehow found their unofficial headquarters.

Another cameraman was directing Rohan: "Can you look slightly betrayed, but still hopeful? Perfect for the thumbnail."

Kabir was busy shielding Simran from the flashing cameras, yelling, "Hey! She's a kindergarten teacher, not a political leader!"

Meher flipped the bird at a paparazzo who got too close, "Zoom in again and I'll rearrange your lens alignment permanently."

And in the very center of this circus stood Rajeev —our sweet, clueless Rajeev — trying to deliver a heartfelt speech.

"What I want to say is... we all must show respect for erection— errr— He Prabhu—I mean, democracy..."

A beat of silence.

Then chaos exploded like a cricket match in a bar.

Aarushi facepalmed so hard she nearly passed out. "I swear," she muttered, "I'm gonna need two law degrees to get us out of this."

9:00 PM — India 24x365 News Debate, "PrimeTime Punch!"

"Namaskar doston!" Priyanka Sehgal's voice blared across living rooms, roadside dhabas, and YouTube livestreams.

"Tonight, we ask the nation — is the rise of people like Rajeev Yadav a threat to democracy... or its unexpected new hope?"

The studio backdrop was an over-the-top swirl of red, gold, and a chaotic collage of stock images — courtrooms, microphones, and... for some reason, a pigeon mid-flight.

Behind the camera, Gogi leaned in and whispered, "Madam, what's the deal with the pigeon? Symbolism or someone just clicked 'select all'?"

Priyanka didn't blink. She straightened her blazer, flashed her million-dollar anchor smile, and declared: "Nation, brace yourself. The circus... has just begun."

The panel was set:

- ➤ Vikas Tyagi (Neta in clean kurta, already prepping hashtags in his head)

- ➤ Advocate Teesta Rawat (hair perfectly blown-out, smelling blood)

- ➤ Random Twitter Activist who ran a "Save Our Culture" page (and had 74 followers)

- ➤ And... Rajeev Yadav himself, sitting awkwardly on the edge of his chair, wearing his best "party shirt" (it had a tiger on it).

Rajeev kept darting nervous glances between the cameras.

"Bhai... am I supposed to look here or there?" he whispered to Gogi. Gogi, lips barely moving, muttered back: "Don't look anywhere. Just sit. Quietly."

Priyanka Sehgal leaned forward, the studio lights catching a glint in her oversized glasses, voice slicing through the dead air like a newsroom guillotine.

"Mr. Rajeev," she said, slow and precise, each syllable sharpened for maximum national outrage.

"You tweeted — and I quote — 'This country needs a proper erection, not dicktaker-ship.'"

She let the words hang like a noose.

"Was that a typo... or a revelation of your true political colors?"

The panelists held their collective breath. Somewhere, a crew member dropped a pen.

The silence wasn't awkward — it was electric.

Rajeev blinked. Twice. Then — for reasons only the gods of comedy could explain — he smiled. A wide, goofy, completely misplaced smile.

Like a schoolkid convinced he just cracked the right answer on a test he never studied for. "Look, madam," he began, puffing his chest slightly, "I fully support democracy from the bottom of my heart."

He tapped his chest for emphasis.

"And by 'erection', I meant..."

(he paused, scanning for validation, none came)

"...I meant standing up — for what's right! Standing tall like— like a... national pole!"

He beamed. The smile of a man who thought he'd just saved the nation and grammar in one breath.

The silence this time was funereal.

Across the studio, anchor Vikas Tyagi fake-coughed into his mic, shoulders trembling with the effort of suppressing laughter. A sound technician choked on his samosa off-camera.

Advocate Teesta Rawat's eyes gleamed. Predator spotted. Kill switch: engaged. She rose like a moral tsunami, brushing an invisible speck from her designer saree, and pounced with the precision of a clickbait headline.

"This—" she thundered, finger jabbing the air like a sentencing wand,

"—isn't just about a slip of tongue. This is about the moral fiber of our society being chewed up by 'influencers' who can't even spell democracy!"

Her voice climbed, like a news ticker spiraling out of control.

Today it's 'erection,' tomorrow it'll be—what? 'Ejaculation for the nation?!'"

The studio gasped. Even Priyanka's perfectly powdered face twitched, as though the phrase had physically slapped her foundation sideways. One panelist let out an audible "Arre baap re..." The intern running subtitles passed out.

And Twitter? Twitter exploded.

#EjaculationForNation started trending in ten minutes.

Kabir, Meher, Rohan, Zayan, and Simran were watching the live broadcast from their chai adda. Meher nearly fell off the bench laughing.

"Our guy Rajeev..." Zayan chuckled, watching the screen. "He's like a full-on public entertainment channel, bro!"

Kabir, still snapping candids, muttered,

"This light... it's tragic. But poetic. Like a Shakespearean mess with chai stains."

—

Back in the studio, Rajeev Yadav — meme material, national joke, trending hashtag incarnate — suddenly leaned forward.

Something in his eyes had shifted. Maybe it was exhaustion. Maybe it was heartbreak in disguise. Maybe, just maybe, it was courage dressed in broken grammar.

He cleared his throat, gripping the edge of the desk like it was a courtroom railing. "Madam," he said, voice trembling with the weight of too many headlines, "English... English is like the stock market."

The room blinked. Priyanka tilted her head, intrigued in spite of herself.

"Always going up… and down," Rajeev continued, hands gesturing wildly, trying to shape metaphors out of thin air.

"But the nation's heart? That should always stay upright. Steady. Straight. No matter what happens."

A pause.

A breath.

And then—

A collective gasp sliced through the studio like a viral retweet. A boom mic wobbled. A crew member choked. In the control room, someone whispered, half-horrified, half-awed:

"Did this man just go full philosopher… with a double meaning?"

What Rajeev had meant was noble. Poetic, even. He meant clarity, truth, moral spine. What it sounded like… was an innuendo explosion sponsored by the universe.

Even Priyanka, seasoned vulture of TRP drama, slapped her notes over her face, shoulders trembling with suppressed hysteria.

And poor Gogi — ever the stoic cameraman — couldn't hold it in anymore. His camera lens dipped mid-shot, shaking violently like it, too, had an opinion.

A slow clap echoed from the far end of the panel.

Vikas Tyagi.

Calm. Composed. Calculating.

"Unorthodox," he said, his voice smooth as news anchor hair gel. "But passionate. And I've always believed it's the heart that makes a true deshbhakt — not diction."

He glanced at Rajeev — not directly, but with the exact warmth of a politician adopting a viral cause just before an election.

Rajeev, blissfully unaware, smiled with the innocence of a man who just delivered what he thought was a TED Talk.

In his mind, he had just dropped a truth bomb.

In the minds of a million viewers — he had just become India's first accidental stand-up philosopher with a pension for suggestive metaphors.

📺 BREAKING GRAPHIC FLASH:

"Is Rajeev Yadav the New Common Man Icon of India?"

Poll: Vote YES or NO!

Meanwhile, memes flooded in:

➢ Rajeev riding a giant dictionary into battle.

➢ Rajeev photoshopped next to Lincoln with the caption "Four erections and seven years ago..."

➢ Rajeev holding a sign: "Make English Great Again."

In the chaos, Rohan quietly posted on Twitter under his secret pen name:

"In a land where typos go viral, truth becomes a typo too."

The tweet mysteriously went viral.

By the time the debate ended, two things were clear:

➢ Rajeev was officially the most lovable, confused national figure since that one guy who mistook Wi-Fi for an energy drink.

➢ Priyanka had just secured her promotion.

Later That Night — It was 1:00 AM, but India's online universe was awake, caffeinated, and bloodthirsty. Under the hashtag #RajeevRocks, every type of internet creature came crawling out:

> ➢ Meme accounts posting Rajeev's confused quotes on sunset wallpapers.

> ➢ Influencers doing "Rajeev Accent Challenges" on Reels: ("Don't be stress, be progress!" while doing yoga poses.)

> ➢ "Intellectual" Twitter debating: "Is bad English the new voice of the oppressed?"

Instagram was hysterical, Twitter was philosophical, and WhatsApp forwards had already declared him the "messiah of the middle class." It wasn't just a viral moment — it was a full-blown social media festival, where irony, sincerity, and absurdity all blurred into one endless scroll.

Meanwhile in a cozy part of Delhi, Aarushi sat cross-legged on her bed, laptop open, half-amused, half-exhausted. She scrolled through a meme that had Rajeev photoshopped as an Avengers superhero — "Captain Democracy: Mispronouncer of Justice."

Aarushi muttered to herself, "Great. This was the only thing left to witness…"

Her phone buzzed.

Message from Rajeev: "Sorry Aarushi. I think I've become the courtroom's leftover sandwich of the day."

She smiled despite herself. Then, with a resigned sigh, she hit call. Rajeev answered nervously, "Hello? Is there… any jail-bail emergency happening?"

Aarushi, trying not to laugh, replied:

"No jail. But if you give one more speech about erections and democracy, I swear I'll personally file a case against you."

Rajeev grinned. "Hey, it's the era of courtship, right? I'm just trying to master legal romance!"

There was a pause. Aarushi rolled her eyes — but smiled wider.

Meanwhile, in the world outside, the chaos only grew:

- ➢ News channels announced "Special Investigations" into Rajeev's life.

- ➢ (One channel even falsely reported he was a dropout from 'Oxford of Outer Kanpur'.)

- ➢ Political WhatsApp groups started spinning fake quotes: "Rajeev Yadav demands National Erection Day!"

- ➢ A random company launched a "Freedom of Speech T-Shirt Collection" with Rajeev's face on it — without his permission.

Amidst the echo of laughter and hashtags, in the middle of courtroom jokes and chai stall chaos, one uncomfortable truth lingered quietly:

That in a country obsessed with perfect pronunciation and spotless image, it often takes a misstep — a typo, a foolish tweet, a clumsy man with a big heart — to remind us that democracy isn't powered by the polished, but by the passionate.

Maybe the real revolution isn't in flawless speeches or viral slogans, but in the courage to speak — especially when the words come out wrong. Because somewhere between mockery and meaning... we find ourselves.

CHAPTER 7

THE NETA & THE NARRATIVE

Morning — Janta Reform Sena Party Office, Gurugram

In a rented 2-room office above a mattress shop — the kind that proudly displayed orthopedic spelled three different ways on three different banners, political ambition was brewing stronger than adrak chai.

Vikas Tyagi, the self-proclaimed face of "Nayi Soch" politics, sat at the head of a plastic table surrounded by whiteboard charts, laptops, and a lot of sweaty idealism.

Just last night, Tyagi had appeared on Priyanka Sehgal's primetime show, nodding gravely through panel chaos while delivering lines like, "Rajeev represents a raw, unfiltered India — the kind that doesn't speak English, but speaks truth."

He hadn't said much, but he'd said it with the confidence of a man who knew silence, too, could be a performance. Twitter called him "measured." His PR team called it a turning point.

On the whiteboard, he wrote:

- ➤ "Engagement > Reality" (underlined twice)
- ➤ "Meme Rajeev = Mass Connect"

Rehan Chaudhary — the social media incharge, meme dealer, and full-time dopamine junkie — burst into the room waving his phone like it was the Constitution itself. His eyes were lit with the feral glow of a man who had just watched a nation lose its mind over a typo.

"Bhaiya!" he yelled, breathless. "The 'dicktaker-ship' meme just crossed one lakh likes. Organic. No boost. Even aunties on Facebook are sharing it with 'Jai Hindi' captions and wrong emojis!"

Vikas Tyagi didn't blink. He was already adjusting the collar of his crisply ironed kurta like a general sharpening his sword before a bloodless coup.

"Good," he murmured. "Now listen carefully."

He leaned forward, palms pressed together like a villain in a biopic pretending to be humble.

"This isn't just a meme anymore. This is sentiment. This is rage wrapped in humour — the most dangerous form of public emotion."

His voice dropped to a whisper. "We don't need policy. We need poetry in failure. A hero not in spite of his mistakes... but because of them."

Rehan's grin widened. "So we spin him as... what? Common man meets comic messiah?"

"No," Vikas said sharply, eyes gleaming.

"We spin him as India's reluctant conscience. A man too raw to be corrupt, too stupid to be strategic — which makes him... perfect."

A silence fell as the gravity of that insanity sank in.

Neetu Bhabhi, lounging nearby in a synthetic saree and sipping Rooh Afza like it was blood wine, looked up from her WhatsApp forwards.

"But bhai saab," she said with mock concern, "what if he says something new? Something even more vulgar? You know how his brain and tongue are permanently divorced."

Balli nodded anxiously. "Or what if he says he's neutral again? That word is very dangerous. Sounds too honest."

Vikas turned to them with the calm malice of a man who'd already planned three outcomes and bought a backup kurta for his arrest photo.

"Balli bhai," he said slowly, "in Indian democracy, no one is truly neutral. They just haven't gone viral yet."

He paused.

"The moment your face becomes a sticker on someone's scooter... your silence belongs to someone else."

Everyone stared.

Then they laughed. Not the laugh of jest, but the laugh of men who knew they were on the edge of turning a meme into a movement — and a mistake into a manifesto.

Vikas leaned back, fingers steepled, already picturing Rajeev's face on campaign hoardings next to slogans like:

"Vote for Voice." "Democracy's Accidental Hero." "Truth. Typo. Triumph."

And somewhere in the distance, a low rumble began — not from the masses but from a printer spitting out the first draft of history, rebranded. Within minutes, the plan was set:

> ➤ Flood Facebook groups with Rajeev memes praising "loktantra is now loksutra ".

> ➤ Create fake quotes supporting "Janta Reform Sena" — attributed to Rajeev.

> ➤ Circulate emotional WhatsApp messages: "A simple, small-time trader raised his voice against tyranny!"

> ➤ Launch a small 'youth rally' outside the court — waving printed posters of Rajeev's face saying: "Vote for Voice!"

Meanwhile, at the Chai Tapri, Rajeev sat munching samosas with Simran and Zayan, completely unaware of the political storm brewing outside.

"You know," he said between bites of chutney-drenched aloo, "maybe I should just try acting…"

Zayan snorted. "Bro, you've already become the Shahrukh Khan of breaking news. Politics might be your next audition."

Rajeev laughed, wiping his fingers. "Politics? I can't even pronounce 'parliament' without panicking!"

As if right on cue, a group of overenthusiastic volunteers in crisp white caps came marching down the lane — waving giant cut-outs of Rajeev's face, chanting with alarming energy: "Hail Rajeev Bhaiya!"

"Real Leader of the Nation — Rajeev Yadav!"

Rajeev choked on his samosa.

"What the hell is happening?!" he gasped.

Simran's eyes widened in disbelief. Zayan, completely unfazed, started recording on his phone. "Welcome to democracy, my friend. Still think anything in life is logical?"

Meanwhile, inside a sleek black SUV parked discreetly nearby, Vikas Tyagi took a slow sip of his black coffee. Watching it all unfold on his tablet, he smiled — calm, calculating. The board was set, and he was already three moves ahead.

Back inside the Tapri, chaos was catching up."Bhaiya! One more chai, please!" Rajeev shouted, voice cracking slightly with panic.

Outside, the chants were growing louder. Someone had even tied a fresh marigold garland around Rajeev's old scooter.

Meher and Kabir came bursting in, breathless and buzzing.

"Rajeev! Bro! You're trending like wildfire!" Meher yelled — half thrilled, half horrified. "Everyone thinks you're joining politics. Some guy even made a poster calling you Desh ka Diler Neta — with your face Photoshopped on Bhagat Singh's body."

Kabir held up his phone:

Trending #3 on Twitter:

- #RajeevForDemocracy
- #VoiceOfThePeople
- #DicktakerShipNoMore

Bro... we've got a problem," Kabir said, eyes still glued to his phone.

Rajeev chuckled nervously.

"Problem? This is free publicity, no? Trending, memes, garlands — feels like a wedding without the bride!"

Kabir didn't blink.

"The problem is... the media thinks you're the youth leader of the opposition party."

Rajeev's grin evaporated. "Wait—what?"

Before he could spiral into full-blown panic, the Tapri door creaked open.

Aarushi entered — black shades on, laptop bag slung over one shoulder, the exact aura of a lawyer who's read ten petitions and hasn't slept in twenty hours. She didn't break stride. Didn't smile. Just said, sharp as a judge's gavel:

"Everyone. Shut up."

The room froze. Even the steam from the chai seemed to pause mid-air. The Tapri fell silent.

Aarushi pulled up a chair, opened her laptop, and projected it toward the group like a courtroom exhibit. On the screen:

India 24x365 Breaking News

"Rajeev Yadav: Accidental Activist or Rising Leader? Inside the viral storm."

There was even a poll running at the bottom:

Would you vote for Rajeev Yadav?

☑ Yes (78%)

✕ No (22%)

Rajeev looked ready to faint. "I just wanted to support democracy," Rajeev whimpered, "even if I spelled it wrong!"

Aarushi rubbed her temples like she was physically holding in a scream.

"Rajeev, you're being used. They're hijacking your face, your words, your chai. If you don't get smart now, you'll end up in either politics... or prison."

Zayan gave a low whistle. "Honestly, both have their own kind of charm."

The glares he received could have melted iron.

Simran looked genuinely shaken.

"Bhaiya, I just wanted to become a school principal... this turned into a revolution!"

Aarushi snapped her laptop shut with a bang. "We need a damage control plan. And fast."

That's when Rohan — quiet, unnoticed till now — finally spoke. Calm. Inevitable.

"First rule of going viral: you don't control the narrative... the narrative controls you."

Everyone turned, stunned. Zayan blinked.

"Bro. Since when did you hide a whole Sun Tzu inside your softboi soul?" Meher muttered.

Rohan just shrugged, sipping his chai calmly.

Meanwhile — Across Town

Inside Vikas Tyagi's SUV, another strategy meeting was happening.

"Let's just organize a rally right outside the court" Neetu Bhabhi suggested, eyes gleaming with excitement like a firecracker ready to pop.

"And we'll get Gogi, the cameraman, to 'accidentally' leak exclusive footage. Trust me — five lakh views in a day, minimum."

Rehan nodded eagerly, already typing hashtags like a man possessed.

Vikas Tyagi didn't say much — he just smiled. That slow, calculating smile of someone watching all the pawns move exactly as planned.

"Operation Hero Rajeev — Phase 2 initiated."

Operation Hero Rajeev

Phase 2 initiated.

CHAPTER 8

YOUR HONOUR, THIS IS A GATED

COMMUNITY!

Location: Tau Hukum Singh's Aangan (courtyard), right next to the Tapri.

Mudpots lined the wall. Plastic chairs creaked under the weight of wisdom, gossip, and growing impatience.

It was an emergency meeting of the RWA Disciplinary Sub-Committee — unofficially known as the Panchayat Plus. The agenda: Should Rajeev and his friends be evicted from the neighbourhood housing block for "bringing shame through vulgarity, political chaos, and too much screen time"?

The media frenzy had reached their gali. News vans had blocked the colony gate. The building's name board had made it to Twitter. And the uncle in flat 203 had complained that his daughter was now asking what erection meant.

Major (Retd.) D.P. Bhalla, the RWA President, sat like a court martial commander in civilian clothes — tall, stiff, and perpetually red in the face, either from rage or rising BP. He wore a cap that said Discipline is Freedom and held a clipboard like it was a charge sheet.

Tau Hukum Singh sat beside him, unofficial advisor and mohalla philosopher. His turban was tilted like a crown and his walking stick rested like a sceptre across his lap. On his other side, Chand Kaur fussed over a giant thermos of chai, while Iqbal Bhai adjusted his ancient spectacles, cleaning them with the edge of his kurta.

Other residents — curious aunties, uncles, and teenagers — gathered around in a rough circle. A hand-painted cardboard read:

"Before Lok Sabha, Mohalla Sabha!"

Rajeev stood in the middle, sweating bullets, while his friends awkwardly lined up behind him like reluctant defense lawyers.

"Bring tea for everyone!" Chand Kaur barked at her grandson. "Discussion without digestion is illegal!"

Aarushi whispered to Rajeev, "Don't speak unless asked. And whatever happens, do not — I repeat — do not attempt English."

Rajeev gulped.

Major Bhalla stood up, cleared his throat like a war announcement was coming.

"In view of recent developments involving explicit language, social media hysteria, and what can only be described as unauthorised virality, this RWA must consider serious disciplinary action. Including — but not limited to — eviction proceedings."

Gasps. Someone dropped a steel glass.

Tau raised a hand, gesturing for silence.

"In this noble assembly of the RWA Disciplinary Sub-Committee" he began, voice slow and thunderous, "we raise a matter of national concern..."

He paused, letting the moment stretch.

"The question is — is Rajeev Yadav the voice of the people... or the doom of the people?"

A few boys at the back couldn't resist — they whistled like it was a Friday matinee. Tau gave a solemn nod and gestured toward Iqbal Bhai.

Iqbal Bhai stood up with the slow gravitas of a retired actor returning for one final scene. He opened a tattered notebook and read aloud, voice rich with judgment:

"Exhibit A: In his tweet, Rajeev used the word 'erection.' Was it a linguistic error... or a question of mental condition?"

Sniggers. Giggles. A coughing fit.

Rajeev, red-faced, mumbled, "It... it was a mistake. Autocorrect did it..."

Chand Kaur cut in, stirring sugar furiously into a giant steel glass like she was mixing revolution with chai.

"Oh, please! I say it was pure love — love for one's motherland! The fault lies in the mobile, not in the man!"

Some elders nodded solemnly. Autocorrect had betrayed many. It was, they agreed silently, an unseen enemy of the people.

Tau leaned forward, eyes twinkling behind his spectacles. "Your tweet sparked a movement, son. Are you ready to carry it forward?"

Rajeev panicked. His heartbeat went into protest mode. Aarushi subtly nudged his leg under the plastic chair. He stood up, hands trembling slightly.

"Tauji... I just... I only wanted to support democracy... and improve—or showcase—my English a little too."

A long, thoughtful silence settled over the courtyard. Dust floated lazily through the air like the moment itself was stalling.

Iqbal Bhai removed his spectacles with ceremonial slowness. "Weak English... but a strong spirit."

Chand Kaur laughed, slapping her knee.

"Just make sure I'm invited to your wedding, son! I want to hear your speech in person!"

Laughter rippled through the gathering like afternoon breeze.

And then — in her soft, sincere voice — Simran spoke up, clutching her little notebook.

"Rajeev Bhaiya always encouraged me in my studies. He's a good person."

A collective "awww" rose from half the mohalla. Even the pigeon on the window cooed in agreement.

Tau lifted his stick and banged it once against the ground like a judge declaring history. The entire courtyard fell silent. The air stiff with anticipation.

Then, he smiled — a slow, mischievous smile.

"English or Hindi, if the emotion is true... language is never a barrier. I hereby declare... Rajeev Yadav the People's Hero of Love!"

The crowd erupted in cheers. Someone set off a cheap firecracker from the nearby gully. Meher whistled loudly. Kabir filmed the whole thing, muttering, "This light... poetic!"

Major Bhalla cleared his throat, but even he couldn't help the smirk creeping across his face.

"Very well," he said gruffly. "Final warning. No more headlines, no more erections... and no interviews without pants."

Rajeev nearly collapsed in relief. Aarushi, standing behind him, smiled for the first time in hours. A real, soft smile — the kind she reserved only for moments that deserved hope.

"Good job, idiot," she whispered.

Rajeev grinned, wiping sweat off his forehead. "Don't be stress, be progress," he muttered back.

They both laughed — maybe too much — as a fresh round of chai arrived and the mohalla turned into a mini carnival

Location: Near the Tapri, behind the Panchayat gathering — hidden, but not hidden enough.

As laughter echoed through the mohalla and garlands found their way around Rajeev's neck, a quieter lens was capturing it all. Priyanka Sehgal adjusted her mic, while Gogi focused the battered news camera toward the chaos. A red LIVE indicator blinked dangerously.

She whispered, almost gleefully, "History is being written... in chai-stained plastic chairs."

Gogi grunted. "And broadcast to eight lakh followers — including two ministers and one confused Bollywood actor."

The shot widened to capture the garlanded "People's Hero" waving like a schoolboy.

Some revolutions start in parliaments.

This one began with a typo and a thermos of chai.

"Chalo chalo, quick bytes nikaalte hain. Jab tak asli news aaye, yahi masala chipka dete hain!" ("Hurry up — let's grab a few quick soundbites. Until real news breaks, this drama will do just fine!") Priyanka barked, slipping effortlessly into her on-camera avatar — all wide eyes, sharper angles, and a voice that could sell war like a bedtime story.

"Viewers," she began, mic held high like a trishul, "in this quiet-looking tea stall courtyard, a new avatar of democracy is taking birth!"

Right on cue, someone burst crackers. A kid flung a packet of gulal into the air. The sky turned a premature pink.

Gogi snorted behind the lens.

"Looks like Holi, Diwali, and Republic Day decided to party together, madam."

Priyanka elbowed him without losing frame, panning the mic toward Chand Kaur, who had now assumed full command over chai distribution like a wartime general rationing caffeine.

"Mataji, what would you like to say about this new youth icon, Rajeev?" Priyanka cooed into the mic, her eyes gleaming with potential headlines.

Chand Kaur gave Rajeev a cheeky wink, then turned to the camera like she'd been waiting for this moment since Doordarshan's black-and-white days.

"Beta Rajeev has heart," she declared, grand and glowing. "He fumbled in English, but he's real from the soul. It's children like him who'll save the country!"

Priyanka nodded like a proud school principal, while mentally drafting viral headlines: From Tweet to Treat: Meet India's Newest Common Man Icon!

Meanwhile, crouched in a corner, Rehan Chaudhary — the digital puppet-master from Vikas Tyagi's team — sneakily filmed the entire scene.

"All we need is one killer caption and a perfect meme," he whispered into his Bluetooth. "Then the views will be ours... and so will the youth."

At the same time, Zayan Khan photobombed the live shot, wearing shades and pretending to be a bodyguard. "No more questions, please. Rajeev Bhai needs rest and coconut water."

Gogi struggled not to laugh.

Across the aangan, Tau Hukum Singh was busy composing a statement of his own — a hand- written note titled:

"Chhoti Angrezi, Badi Soch."

He handed it to Iqbal Bhai for corrections ("where is Comma, tauji?"), while Chand Kaur posed for selfies with passing schoolgirls.

In the middle of all this, Rajeev just stood there — dazed, overwhelmed, and somehow... weirdly happy.

Aarushi slid up next to him, whispering: "You're officially a movement now. God help us all."

Rajeev turned to her, eyes shining. "All I wanted was to stand by democracy... but now it feels like I am the democracy — being pulled, punched, and paraded!"

Kabir caught the moment on camera — the awkward hero of a very awkward revolution. And at that exact second, the hashtags exploded:

#RajeevForRajyaSabha

#ChotiAngreziBadiSoch

#TapriRevolution

The Chai Chronicles were no longer just seven friends at a weekend tapri.

They had — unintentionally — become the heartbeat of a very confused nation. A nation that scrolled for outrage, shared for irony, and accidentally crowned heroes between chai breaks and trending hashtags.

CHAPTER 9

CTRL+ALT+DEFAME

Location: Later that Night – Outside the Tapri

The energy was finally starting to settle, but the air still buzzed with the aftertaste of revolution. Bits of marigold petals clung to clothes, slogans still echoed faintly down the alley, and a camera light blinked sleepily, forgotten on the footpath.

The Chai Chronicles crew sat in a quiet huddle around a steaming kettle, trying to process what had just happened.

Rajeev, still in a mild state of shellshock, looked down at the crate he'd used as a podium and muttered, "Long live democracy... and for the record, I officially end the Great Chutney War of our mohalla — red and green, equal rights. This nation has space for all flavours, all voices."

He paused, then added with a dazed grin, "Bhai, I think I just launched a political party... with chutneys and punchlines."

Rohan chuckled. "With pickles for funding and spelling mistakes as the manifesto."

Their Chand Biji had, by now, officially declared the launch of a 'Rajeev Support Fund' — powered by jars of homemade achaar. She was already arguing over label designs with the neighborhood printer.

Aarushi, now hunched over her phone, was furiously drafting a pre-emptive legal strategy with her friends from NLU.

"We need to get ahead of this before the court thinks you're leading an uprising," she said without looking up.

Kabir added, "And definitely before Major Bhalla sends an RWA notice accusing you of weaponising chutney."

Location: 5 AM – The Next Morning, Aarushi's Room

Aarushi was already awake — not that she'd really slept. She'd spent the night scrolling through headlines that swung wildly between mockery and martyrdom:

> ➢ Rajeev Yadav: Rebel Without a Grammar Check?

> ➢ Tweet Kranti: Is This India's Most Accidental Leader?

> ➢ #MurgiAchaarMovement Trending in 4 States

She sipped her black coffee like it was armor. "This isn't just court optics anymore. It's political theatre."

The NLU Natives group buzzed: Need full timeline, emotional damage angle, plus media bias examples. We'll wrap it in a 'Free Speech vs Misinterpretation' argument — punchy but defensible.

Aarushi replied with a thumbs-up, then looked at Rajeev, who was still asleep — clutching a pillow like it owed him a vote, mumbling something about "draft speeches" in his sleep.

She shook her head, equal parts lawyer, babysitter, and accidental campaign manager — but beneath the exasperation, a flicker of worry crept in.

This wasn't just a meme anymore. It was real, and it had consequences.

Location: Meher's Living Room

A former drawing room, now repurposed as a temporary war bunker — chosen not for comfort, but for its excellent WiFi and the fact that it was three lanes away from reporters, chai mobs, and anyone with a microphone.

No news vans. No slogans. No unexpected garlanding.

Just four walls, dusty curtains, and enough silence for a group of very tired revolutionaries to finally think.

The table was a war zone of biscuit crumbs, printouts, half-eaten samosas, and one emergency bottle of hajmola.

Everyone looked like they hadn't slept in days. Because they hadn't.

Rajeev sat in the middle, eyes wild, hair wilder, clutching a newspaper with his face Photoshopped onto a lion's body.

Headline: "Simbaa of Swatantrata?"

"This is not even my body type," he mumbled.

Kabir was scrolling through Twitter.

"Bro, you're trending alongside onions and a leaked minister's dance video."

Zayan sighed. "One of those things has layers. Spoiler: it's not you."

Meher, who had just returned from attempting to stop someone from printing Vote for Erection T-shirts, slammed down a stack of flyers.

"They're using your name to sell chai-flavoured condoms now. The slogan is 'Taste the Revolution'!"

Simran blinked. "I don't even know what that means, but I'm disturbed."

Rohan, ever the quiet volcano, closed his laptop and looked up. "They're hijacking the story. Not just your face or your English. Your whole... vibe."

Aarushi walked in, holding two cups of chai and her usual look of caffeinated wrath.

"Update: Your hearing is tomorrow. You know, the actual court case we forgot because you got too busy becoming a revolution."

Rajeev groaned.

"But... Aarushi... if people is liking me now, won't the judge also... you know... feel my vibe?"

Aarushi nearly dropped her chai.

"The judge does not give relief for vibe! This is not Instagram."

Zayan raised a finger. "I mean... if we hashtag it cleverly—"

"No!" Aarushi barked. "No more hashtags. No more rallies. No more posters. From now till the hearing, we do damage control. Serious mode."

Simran raised her hand timidly.

"Should we cancel the puppet show we planned outside the court then?"

Everyone turned.

Simran shrunk back.

"It was supposed to be educational... with sock puppets... about Article 19."

Aarushi took a deep breath, then sipped her chai like it was a sedative.

Kabir finally looked up.

"We need to reset. This whole thing... it started because Rajeev tweeted from the heart. Now he's a sticker, a slogan, a Saturday news cycle."

Meher nodded. "We're not fighting the system anymore. We're doing item numbers for it."

Zayan: "Bro, we are the item number."

Aarushi stood up, full lawyer mode.

"Tomorrow, we go to court. No drama. No slogans. No sock puppets. Just facts, law, and basic grammar. Or at least... basic spell check."

Rajeev raised his hand meekly.

"What about one small poster? Just one? With like... emotional font?"

Aarushi glared.

"Okay. No poster. Only truth. Truth is my poster."

She paused. Smiled. "Almost there, Mr. Erection. Almost."

And then, as if summoned by fate and WiFi, Rohan turned his laptop toward them all. "Rajeev — you need to say something. Publicly. Before they finish printing your face on party flags."

Rajeev stood, cleared his throat like a man about to read his own eulogy, and hit "Go Live" on Instagram.

"Namaste India. This is Rajeev Yadav — also known as typo king, English struggler, and currently, wrongly assumed neta.

I just want to say... I am not a part of Vikas Tyagi's party. I am not part of any party. I am party of mango people.

My mistake went viral. But now some people are trying to make that mistake into movement. Into politics. Into TRP. But my intention was never that. I just wants better country. Not banner with my face.

So please... keep your votes. I only wants bail."

The video ended. It buffered. It exploded.

Within minutes:

- #RajeevClearsIt
- #NoToTyagiYesToChai
- #ErectionForBail trended — again.

But something shifted.

For the first time, Rajeev had spoken clearly — if not in grammar, then in heart.

And so, in Meher's battle-scarred living room, surrounded by cracked phones, chai mugs, and friends who refused to let a typo turn into tragedy, they prepared for court.

Not as memes. Not as messiahs.

But as mildly chaotic citizens... trying to Ctrl+Z their way to redemption.

Outside Rajnagar Nyayalaya, a makeshift media pen had already formed.

Cameramen were doing stretches. A news anchor from "Desh Tak" applied compact powder while mumbling, "Hope he says something stupid again."

Simran arrived with a box of achaar jars, whispering, "Just for moral support."

Balli wore sunglasses and kept saying, "No comments at this time," to every pedestrian, including a paanwala.

Tau Hukum Singh, Chand Kaur, Iqbal Bhai and others also wanted to support their local hero. They sat waiting under the sacred banyan tree, debating whether to submit a character certificate for Rajeev to the court.

"I say we submit video footage of his school poetry competition from Class 4," said Chand Kaur proudly. "He said 'India is my mother, I am her tea.'"

Iqbal Bhai corrected her gently. "It was 'I am her tree.' But let the record reflect his passion."

Tau nodded. "This is a new freedom struggle. Our boy is fighting for every mohalla misfit who couldn't spell 'constitutional crisis' but lived it anyway."

Inside the Court Premises, the judge hadn't even entered, but murmurs were already swirling: "Public nuisance or public figure?", "Incitement or accident?", "Are pickles legally admissible as political expression?"

Aarushi pulled Rajeev aside. "From this moment on, every word matters. No improv. No emotion. Just legalese."

Rajeev gulped. "So... no mention of chutney?"

"Especially no mention of chutney."

The opposite counsel, Teesta Rawat, was already basking in her newfound spotlight — like a peacock in protest mode.

She faced the cameras with a perfectly practiced scowl and declared, "This is about more than one man. This isn't about a typo — it's about accountability. We cannot excuse ignorance as activism. When language is misused in the public domain, it misleads millions. Free speech comes with responsibility — not just viral hashtags."

Aarushi rolled her eyes. "She's using you as a symbol."

Rajeev nodded. "Cool. As long as symbols don't go to jail." Rajeev adjusted the collar of his kurta, heart pounding.

Aarushi straightened his sleeves like a reluctant campaign manager fixing her candidate.

"You ready?" she asked.

"No," he replied. "But I've got a good lawyer, emotional support pickles, and apparently, a fanbase."

The courtroom door creaked open.

History, or at least a very chaotic court record, was about to be made.

CHAPTER 10

TRENDING IN SESSION

By now, Rajnagar Nyayalaya didn't need another introduction — everyone in the country had probably seen it in a meme.

But today, Courtroom No. 3 had a different kind of buzz. Not the usual property dispute or stolen scooter case — today, it was hosting a potential constitutional crisis powered by autocorrect.

The room crackled with anticipation. Law students with unpaid internships had shown up just for gossip. A YouTuber disguised as a paralegal was livestreaming from behind a stack of files.

Manoj Bhaiya, the bailiff, lazily called out names like a bored wedding DJ.

"Petition for Quashing FIR — Rajeev Yadav versus State of Twitter Disgrace... I mean State of India!" He announced, then muttered under his breath, "What all one has to endure, dear God..."

Someone in the back coughed loudly to cover their laughter. Even the stenographer rolled their eyes.

At the front, behind a mighty (and slightly cracked) wooden bench, sat Hon'ble Justice V.P. Mishra — wearing his thick glasses, scowling at his mobile phone.

"What is this 'hashtag' thing? And under which law does a 'meme' fall?" he grumbled to himself, flipping through the file.

He looked up sharply as Aarushi walked in, crisp and composed, files in hand. Behind her, Rajeev nervously followed, wearing the borrowed coat that looked like it belonged to a retired magician.

Kabir, Meher, Zayan, Simran, and Rohan filed into the back benches like obedient schoolkids — Team Rajeev.

Meanwhile, across the room, Advocate Teesta Rawat — sharp as a sword in a power saree — adjusted her microphone, smiling for the news cameras peeking through the cracked window.

Win or lose today, she had already secured her next headline. Just that morning, she'd drafted a fresh PIL titled:

"Preserving Linguistic Decency and Democratic Dignity: The Need to Regulate Public Figures' Social Media Conduct."

Because if justice didn't go her way, relevance still could.

The courtroom vibe was pure circus now — part Kavi Sammelan, part reality show, and part mock parliament, with just enough legalese to pretend it was serious.

Judge Mishra cleared his throat. "Present your case."

Teesta pounced forward: "Milord, we live in a digital democracy. And language is the foundation of a civil society. When citizens like Mr. Rajeev Yadav tweet grossly incorrect English mixed with subversive political opinions, it leads to confusion, chaos, and corrosion of cultural values!"

Cue dramatic gasp from a planted audience member.

Judge Mishra adjusted his glasses.

"Are you saying that the culture of India can be shaken by a drunk tweet?"

Teesta, undeterred, nodded solemnly. "Yes, Milord. It's a question of public morality."

From the back row, Meher crossed her arms and muttered just loud enough for the group to hear: "Amazing. Murder accused roam free, but typo criminals? Straight to trending and trial."

Zayan leaned over, whispering, "Say it louder for the judge. I don't think he heard you."

Aarushi, without turning around, held up one finger like a traffic signal: Do. Not. Poke. The. Bear.

The group went silent again — but the sarcasm had already served its purpose. A crack in the courtroom tension.

Rajeev, confused, leaned toward Aarushi and whispered: "Which section of the IPC does this so-called morality fall under? 302 or 420?"

Aarushi closed her eyes briefly, as if summoning strength from the legal gods. She rose with quiet authority, her voice calm but cutting as she began her counter.

"Milord, my learned friend has confused grammatical errors with criminal intent. My client's tweet, while...unfortunate in language, was a legitimate expression of democratic concern. If we start policing bad English, Milord, half the internet will be in jail, including some elected representatives."

Half the courtroom snorted. Even Justice Mishra's moustache twitched.

"Valid point, Advocate Malhotra," he murmured.

Meanwhile, Pinky the clerk typed furiously on her typewriter, pausing only to giggle when Rajeev mispronounced "Constitution" as "Construction."

In the back, Zayan whispered: "If bad English came with a fine, we'd all be throwing a party behind bars."

Kabir clicked a discreet photo of Rajeev sweating buckets and captioned it: "Breaking: Local man fights for democracy with broken grammar." (Uploaded to Insta story: #OurHero #NoFilterNeeded)

Meher smacked his arm. "Delete it, idiot. Aarushi will be fighting your case next."

Judge Mishra tapped the table with his pen.

"Enough entertainment. I need legal precedents. Show me the law violated, or this case is a waste of state resources!"

Teesta dramatically flipped open a 500-page book — some obscure constitutional commentary she'd borrowed just for the drama.

Aarushi calmly sipped water. Rajeev stared at the ceiling fan, mentally composing his next apology tweet.

Outside the courtroom, more reporters and chai vendors gathered, sensing a historic verdict brewing.

And thus began the hungama — the full legal tamasha of #RajeevKoNyay.

The air had turned serious now. Rajeev sat quietly at the petitioner's bench, his energy finally drained.

Aarushi looked over at him, catching that rare glimpse: the real Rajeev — not the meme, not the joke, but the boy from Kanpur who genuinely loved his country... in his own awkward, broken-English way.

Elsewhere, in newsrooms across India, anchors were already prepping split-screen debates:

"Hero or Hype?", "Can One Typo Start a Revolution?", "Is English the New Oppressor?"

On a channel with dramatic music and flaming text, a pundit yelled: "This is not just a legal issue — this is a cultural war between commas and karma!"

Nobody knew what the verdict would be yet. But TRPs had already reached a unanimous decision: Rajeev was gold.

Back in the courtroom — Aarushi stood up, her voice steady:

"Milord, in a nation where freedom of speech is protected under Article 19, where democracy thrives on diversity of opinion, how can a typing error — however humorous — be treated as sedition, nuisance, or obscenity?"

Judge Mishra tapped his pen thoughtfully.

Aarushi continued: "My client, Rajeev Yadav, is not a criminal. He is a symbol — of thousands of Indians who dare to participate in the digital discourse without perfect grammar, without perfect polish... but with perfect intent."

You could feel the shift in the courtroom.

Even Advocate Teesta Rawat, arms crossed, had to admit: Aarushi was good.

Aarushi added, soft but firm:

"English is not — and should never become — the currency for judging patriotism or purity of thought."

Kabir whispered under his breath: "Mic drop."

Suddenly, Rajeev stood up impulsively. Aarushi hissed, "Sit. Down." But he couldn't.

With slightly trembling hands, Rajeev folded them respectfully and spoke: "Milord, I just want to say one thing.

I may be weak in English — but not in intention.

If my tweet hurt anyone, I sincerely apologize.

But I love my country, my democracy, and my people — with all my heart."

There was a pause. A pause so full, it swallowed every meme, every whisper.

Even Advocate Teesta lowered her stack of papers for a moment.

Justice Mishra peered over his glasses, eyes suddenly sharp and unreadable.

"So... you do understand the power of words, Mr. Yadav?"

Rajeev nodded — like a schoolboy caught but not crushed, standing tall before the principal.

"Very good," the judge murmured.

And the silence deepened, this time with something else: A strange, swelling respect.

Judge Mishra adjusted his glasses and cleared his throat. "Advocate Rawat, any rebuttal?"

Teesta stood, less aggressive now.

"Milord, my concern is only that viral mistakes affect public behavior. We must promote responsible speech."

Judge Mishra nodded: "Responsible speech, yes. Responsible outrage, even more so."

He leaned forward, eyes twinkling. "Court will now pronounce a special verdict."

Rajeev gulped.

Judge Mishra opened a thick, leather-bound diary. Everyone leaned in. And he read aloud:

"Bhasha galat ho sakti hai, bhavna nahi.

Angrezi mein fissalna, rashtrabhakti mein nahin.

Galat tweet se na rashtra tootta hai, na sapne toot te hain.

Jo tweet karta hai, woh sochta hai. Jo sochta hai, who zinda hai."

(Language can be wrong, but emotions cannot. To slip in English is not to slip in patriotism. A wrong tweet does not destroy a nation or dreams. The one who tweets, thinks. The one who thinks, is alive.)

A stunned pause.

The courtroom burst into light applause — even Manoj Bhaiya clapped twice before stopping awkwardly.

The Judgment Speech:

"In this country, we have freedom of speech," Justice Mishra began — voice calm, deliberate.

"But with every freedom comes responsibility."

Everyone listened — still, breath held.

"Rajeev Yadav's tweet... was inappropriate. There was carelessness in the choice of words. But there was no criminal intent behind it. It was a mistake. Not an act of malice."

Rajeev blinked rapidly, heart pounding.

Justice Mishra went on:

"Therefore, this Court — in the interest of justice, awareness, and reform — quashes the FIR filed against Rajeev Yadav, with a directive to undertake community service as a constructive consequence. Let this be an opportunity for learning, not punishment."

Murmurs erupted like waves through the courtroom.

Aarushi exhaled — slow, controlled — the kind of relief only lawyers and hostage negotiators understood.

Rajeev, unsure whether to cheer or bow, simply whispered, "Does this mean I'm free... or employed?"

Leaning toward Aarushi, whispering, "So... no jail?"

Aarushi gave a faint smile. "No jail, Rajeev. Just some community service."

From the back, Kabir leaned in with a wicked grin. "Bhai, You'll be teaching English."

Rajeev looked up at the ceiling, as if he'd just had a direct conversation with the divine.

Before leaving, Justice Mishra paused, his gaze resting squarely on Rajeev, his voice carrying a gentle gravity.

"Young people like you must understand — On social media, a grammar mistake might be forgiven...But a mistake of intent will not."

He paused — then added, with a knowing smile: "And yes, next time... don't blame autocorrect. Keep both your brain and heart switched on."

Court dismissed.

A collective sigh of relief swept through the courtroom like a breeze after a storm. Outside, Priyanka Sehgal was already facing the camera, mic raised, script in mind:

"The English Murder: Justice Served — with a Lesson in Heart."

Zayan pretended to wipe a tear. Meher high-fived Kabir.

Simran hugged Aarushi tightly.

Rajeev looked at Aarushi, a bit teary-eyed himself.

"Thank you, Aarushi. If it weren't for you... I'd probably be sitting in jail writing poetry by now."

Aarushi smirked: "Saved just in time. Otherwise, 'jailhouse erection' would've been the next trending tweet!"

They both laughed — the first real laugh they shared since the storm began.

Outside, the media vans swarmed, but for now, inside that crumbling courthouse, it was only friendship, relief, and second chances that mattered.

Cut to the familiar clinking of steel glasses, the smell of cardamom chai in the air.

Tau Hukum Singh, Chand Kaur, and Iqbal Bhai had already secured their "VIP seats" on the bench.

As Rajeev walked in, the entire group at the tea stall — locals, elders, kids playing cricket — clapped for him.

"What kind of leader do we want? One like Rajeev Bhaiya!" someone joked.

Rajeev, blushing to the roots, folded his hands in a namaste, his voice cracking:

"Thank you, public. From now on, I'll tweet responsibly... and yes, I'll make sure autocorrect is ON before I start a revolution!"

Everyone erupted with laughter.

Simran rushed forward and hugged him tight. "Bhaiya, you were so brave!"

Kabir clicked a candid — Rajeev mid-hug, teary-eyed, with Simran grinning wide.

Meher slapped Rajeev's back: "Fine, now go get it tattooed on your arm: THINK BEFORE YOU TWEET."

Zayan added, "And yes, don't forget to enroll in English tuition too — revolution ke saath grammar correction free milega!" ("With every revolution, you get free grammar correction!")

Pinky from the court clerk's office also passed by, holding Maggi packets, and winked: "Good job, Advocate Aarushi!"

Aarushi simply nodded, cool and composed — but her eyes were sparkling with something deeper: pride. Relief. Maybe... a little bit of something else too.

They all settled into their usual table — seven steel glasses, seven plates of Maggi.

Aarushi sat next to Rajeev, unusually quiet.

He leaned towards her, whispering:

"You know... when the judge was reciting that poem... I wasn't listening to him.

I was looking at you."

Aarushi arched an eyebrow: "What else did you see?"

Rajeev smiled, earnest and unfiltered: "I saw that when the whole world was laughing at me...you were the only one fighting for me."

Aarushi's sarcasm defenses crumbled for a second. She stared into her chai.

Rajeev fumbled, scratching his head:

"I mean... what I'm trying to say is... you're the best. That's it. Just the best."

The group noticed the vibe shift but tactfully chose to ignore it. Kabir announced "Victory photo time!"

They huddled together, messy, noisy, warm. Click.

A photo that would later hang in each of their hearts, even when times would change.

Meanwhile across the street, Priyanka Sehgal signed off her live coverage:

"Viewers, today, a wrongly worded English tweet has turned a small-town boy into a national superstar! This is the true color of the new India."

Gogi the cameraman muttered under his breath: "And the real heroes are chai and friendship, madam."

As the sun set over Rajnagar, painting the sky in orange and pink, Rajeev looked around at his friends, his family of misfits, and thought:

"Maybe my English is broken. But today, my life feels... perfectly repaired."

CHAPTER 11

PROOFREAD MY HEART

Scene: Night. Aarushi's apartment in Gurugram, dimly lit and quiet — the kind of quiet that comes only after chaos has passed, but not fully settled.

The gang had gone their separate ways after the court verdict, promising to meet again soon. But Rajeev... he couldn't leave. Not yet.

He stood awkwardly outside Aarushi's door, holding a box of her favorite soan papdi (the cheap kind from the corner shop — he didn't know what else to bring).

He was about to knock when the door opened.

Aarushi stood there — in an oversized T-shirt, hair in a messy bun, no courtroom armor, no sarcasm mask. Just her.

" You're back?" she said, simply.

Rajeev (softly, with a smile): "I never left...

I was just lingering in the pauses of your breath,

waiting in the silence between your sentences.

Even when I was far, I was only a thought away—

a typo in your heart's rough draft... still unfinished, still yours."

Aarushi's living room smelled like lemon-scented floor cleaner and burnt popcorn. The TV played some mindless singing competition at low volume.

Aarushi plopped down on the couch and motioned for him to sit too.

"You planning to sit there all day, or actually say something useful in this courtroom?" she teased, raising an eyebrow.

Rajeev sat — on the very edge — like a schoolboy waiting for parent-teacher scolding. Aarushi stared at him for a few seconds.

Long enough to make Rajeev fidget.

Finally, she spoke — voice steady but... soft.

"Rajeev... tujhe pata hai kya hua aaj?" ("Rajeev... do you even realise what happened today?")

He blinked.

"Yes, I got bail."

"And?" she asked, eyebrows arched in quiet challenge.

"And... the judge didn't make fun of my English."

Aarushi shook her head, a slow smile playing on her lips.

"And... you got a chance to stay alive. To change yourself—without losing who you are."

Rajeev looked at his hands. "But I only said election... who the hell slipped 'erection' in between?"

He said it so earnestly that Aarushi couldn't help laughing — a bright, beautiful laugh that filled the room.

When she stopped, she looked at him — seriously this time.

"Rajeev," she said, "I don't want to change you. I just want that when the world laughs at you... you don't laugh along. I want you to understand yourself. To love yourself. Because this world? It was never smart enough to understand you anyway."

Rajeev swallowed hard. No joke came to his lips. No funny line.

Just silence. Real, raw silence.

And something cracked open inside him — The boy who had learned to hide behind bad English and worse jokes... was finally seen.

Without thinking, Rajeev reached for her hand. Aarushi didn't pull away.

She squeezed back. No words. No confessions. No declarations. Just a simple, solid truth between them: We're in this together.

Outside, a cool wind blew over the city of dreams and mistakes.

Inside, Rajeev Yadav — the Confident Clown — had finally found someone who didn't laugh at him. And maybe... just maybe... loved him too.

Time slipped by quietly, as if even the universe didn't want to interrupt.

The clock ticked past midnight.

Now, Rajeev and Aarushi sat shoulder to shoulder on the couch, a half-eaten packet of soan papdi between them — the only witness to a night that didn't need words to matter.

No chaos. No noise.

Just two people... breathing a little easier because the world outside had stopped mattering for a while.

Aarushi tilted her head, studying Rajeev as he stared out the window.

"What are you thinking?" she asked. Rajeev shrugged.

"I'm just thinking... if I were the king of English... spoke in an Oxford accent... maybe the world would've taken me seriously from the start, no?"

Aarushi gave a small, sad smile.

"Rajeev," she said, her voice steady, "When a person has true strength, it's not language that proves it—it's their work."

Rajeev let out a dry chuckle. "Work? All I do is set up tents at weddings. Blow up balloons.

People say... 'Is that even a real job?' But what can I do, Aarushi? This is all I know."

He turned to look at her, eyes shining with something between defiance and defeat.

"I want to dream, but even dreams demand English these days."

Aarushi reached out and placed her hand on his chest — over his heart.

"Look here. This doesn't ask for a degree, nor a dictionary."

Rajeev laughed — a short, broken sound.

"You're a lawyer. You can talk about big, important things. I'm just a funny guy... who went viral by accident."

Aarushi leaned in, her voice low, almost a whisper.

"It wasn't an accident. It was the truth. Your tweet — no matter how chaotic — came from the heart. And the truth... sometimes it feels like a mistake, but it never is."

Rajeev blinked quickly, trying to seem normal, manly, unaffected. He failed miserably. He looked at Aarushi.

"What if I... want to become something else?"

"Then become it."

"But what?" he asked, genuinely lost.

Aarushi smiled — a slow, patient smile, like she had all the time in the world.

"Whatever makes you happy. Whether it's politics, or setting up wedding mandaps. Whether it's doing comedy on Twitter. Or even just... you and me, with a cup of tea, sitting the whole day together.

The TV, forgotten in the background, played some emotional score — as if it, too, could feel the shift in the air.

Rajeev found himself whispering:

"What if I lose you in all this?"

Aarushi gently squeezed his hand.

"Dream of winning me. Not of losing me."

A silence followed — heavy, profound, brimming with meanings too large for language.

And then, without ceremony, without any filmy buildup — Rajeev leaned forward and kissed her forehead.

Simple. Pure. Trembling.

The kind of kiss that said: "Thank you for seeing me... when even I couldn't see myself."

Aarushi closed her eyes, letting the moment seep into her skin, anchoring itself somewhere deep.

Outside, the city roared with ambition, breaking news, and trending hashtags. Inside, two people discovered that maybe... the real revolution wasn't out there. Maybe it was always within them.

In the murder of wrong English, of broken dreams, and battered hopes —something beautiful was born.

Love.

Unscripted.

Unapologetic. Unstoppable.

Morning sunlight crept into Aarushi's tiny living room, casting golden streaks across forgotten teacups, half-eaten chips, and crumpled paper napkins — quiet echoes of a night that had been anything but.

But amidst the mess, two things stood out clearly — Rajeev and Aarushi, asleep side-by-side on the couch, her head on his shoulder, his arm loosely around her.

It was innocent. It was soft. It was scandalous — at least for their nosy friends.

Meher lit a beedi, her eyes gleaming with mischief. "Ayy, so this was the hidden plot twist? You pulled off a major setting, Rajeev Bhaiya!"

Zayan grinned wickedly. "Breaking News: Rajeev Bhaiya's English — slain. Aarushi Di's heart — captured."

Simran clutched her heart dramatically, like a Sooraj Barjatya heroine. "Haww! Bhaiya and Di! So wholesome, so filmi!"

Rohan, ever calm, sipped his chai and murmured, "Some people are quietly writing their love story... and here we are, busy making memes."

The group exchanged looks — the kind packed with a thousand unspoken jokes, buried emotions, and enough future blackmail material to last a lifetime.

The Ambush

Meher tiptoed toward the couch like a hunter stalking rare prey, her phone camera already rolling.

Kabir noticed and hissed, "Bro, don't do it. He'll feel bad."

Meher smirked without looking back. "Exactly. That's why we'll get the best angle."

She leaned in. Click-click-click.

Rajeev stirred awake, blinking at the sudden light. At first, he smiled sleepily—then froze.

There they were: a full audience, phone cameras raised, faces brimming with mischievous grins.

He shot up, panicked. "Hey... hey... it's nothing! We were just... uh... brainstorming!"

Zayan couldn't resist. "Brainstorming? Or heart-storming?"

Meher flashed the phone screen proudly. "What do you think the caption should be? 'From trending tweets to trending hearts'?"

Aarushi, now fully awake and sitting up, threw them all a death glare sharp enough to win a standing ovation in any courtroom. Her voice was calm, cold, and lethal:

"I can file a privacy infringement suit against all of you."

The room went silent. Everyone backed off instantly—laughing nervously, but just a little scared.

But beneath the teasing, the gang felt it. Something had changed. Something real had settled into place.

Rajeev and Aarushi weren't just flirting anymore. They weren't just friends in crisis.

They were... something else now. Something solid. Honest.

Later, Simran leaned toward Rohan and whispered, "They needed each other, na?"

Rohan nodded, his voice soft. "Like all of us. We quietly take care of each other... even if we never say it out loud."

Outside, the world still saw Rajeev as a walking typo — the accidental poster boy for misplaced grammar. But in this room, at this table, he was more.

A fighter. A friend. A lover. Their brother.

And someone who finally believed he deserved better than being everyone's punchline — someone ready to rewrite his story on his own terms.

CHAPTER 12

THE CHAI CHRONICLES: FINAL BREW

One year later. New lives, same madness.

The sun blazed over the Delhi-Gurgaon border, now dustier but somehow livelier than before.

The same tea stall stood proudly in place; its wooden planks freshly painted a faded blue. The plastic chairs were still cracked, the chai still too sweet, and the conversations as chaotic as ever. Some things, thankfully, never changed.

The Chai Chronicles table was fully occupied once again.

Rajeev Yadav (@FinallyLearning95) had changed his handle.

Gone was the infamous @ProudRajeev95 and with it, the era of accidental meme stardom. After the courtroom drama, Rajeev had become something of a minor celebrity in his area, invited to inaugurate everything from yoga camps to vegetable markets.

But today, he was just another boy at the tapri, wearing a slightly crumpled kurta and holding Aarushi's hand under the table like a nervous teenager.

He still said things like, "Don't be stress, be progress." But now he said it while genuinely studying English through a free online course. Because now, he truly believed he was worth the effort.

Aarushi Malhotra remained the boss lady, though her world had changed too. She had resigned from her cut-throat Delhi law firm six months ago. Now she worked independently—focusing on pro bono cases, women's rights, and education reforms.

Her Instagram bio read: "Lawyer. Dreamer. Partner-in-Crime (and grammar) to one English Warrior."

Every time Rajeev butchered a proverb, she still facepalmed. Secretly, she loved it. It was their language now.

Kabir Khanna had finally confessed to Meher.

She responded, "Let's ruin each other's lives slowly." The two were now officially listed as "complicated" on Facebook.

Kabir took photos, Meher inked tattoos, and somehow they understood each other without needing fancy captions. He even framed a photo of Rajeev's original tweet and hung it in his studio under the title: "Where Chaos Meets Courage."

Meher Qureshi had opened her second tattoo studio. She still smoked beedis, still lovingly punched people.

For reasons no one could explain, she tattooed Rajeev's corrected slogan on Kabir's arm: "This country needs a proper election, not a dictatorship. Jai Hind." Spelling double-checked by Aarushi.

Rohan Sharma had finally published his first novel—anonymously. It became a sleeper hit among college kids: a love story about a boy who tweets his way into revolution.

The dedication read: "To the fools who dream and the friends who make it worth it." (He had also mostly moved on from his crush on Aarushi... mostly.)

Simran Batra had started her own village school with the help of crowdfunding. She named it "Udaan - School of Second Chances."

She still baked, still hugged too tight, still cried too easily. At the school's inauguration, she called Rajeev her "biggest idiot and best inspiration," and the whole village cried along.

Zayan Khan was still smooth-talking and still single.

He had started a YouTube comedy channel called Zayan Speaks. His viral skit, "How English Murdered Our Friendship (But We Laughed Anyway)," featured dramatic reenactments of Rajeev's journey—all approved (and heavily roasted) by Rajeev himself.

Priyanka Sehgal and Gogi had finally left India 24x365.

They started a satirical YouTube news channel: News That's Actually True. Their first headline? "Local Boy Teaches Country Importance of English, Friendship, and Grammar (Not in That Order)."

Judge V.P. Mishra had re-retired with full honours.

He wrote a poetry book titled: Justice vs. Nonsense. It became a cult favourite among law students. In his last interview, when asked about Rajeev's case, he smiled and said, "At times, justice speaks the language of the heart—not English."

And the Chai Spot?

Still buzzing with laughter and gossip.

As the sun dipped below the dusty trees, Rajeev stood up and raised his chai cup high. "Everyone! We've got ourselves a fresh new word!"

Groans erupted around the table.

Rajeev, grinning like a mad poet, declared, "Progresstination: when you delay, but at least you smile while delaying!"

Everyone burst out laughing. Chai cups clinked. Beedis flared. The sun set.

Their English might still murder dictionaries. Their lives might still be messy. But somehow, they had all survived.

And they had learned the most important language of all: Love, Friendship, and Second Chances.

THE END.

AFTERWORD

(A cup of chai for your thoughts.)

Stories are funny things.

Sometimes, they begin with a grand plan — maps, outlines, perfect dialogues.

And sometimes... they begin with a typo at 2:12 AM.

The English Murder was never just about broken English.

It was about broken hearts stitched back together. About foolish dreams that somehow survived. About a group of people who — despite all odds — chose laughter over loneliness,

hope over cynicism, and friendship over fame.

Rajeev, Aarushi, Kabir, Meher, Rohan, Simran, Zayan — they were never perfect. They lied, they fought, they misunderstood each other.

But they showed up. Every weekend.

Over endless cups of chai, cheap plastic chairs, and badly spelled WhatsApp groups.

Maybe that's all life really asks of us:

Show up. Laugh at yourself. Fight for your people. And when you fail (because you will), try again — with a little less pride and a lot more love.

This story ends here.

But somewhere, maybe right now, a new group of idiots is forming — planning protests, plotting dreams, sipping over-sweet chai, and mispronouncing "democracy."

May their English be wild.

May their friendships be wilder.

And may they always find their way home — no matter how messy the map.

Thank you for reading. Thank you for believing.

See you at the next tea stall.

ACKNOWLEDGEMENTS

(*Written by Rajeev Yadav*)

Hello respected and non-respected peoples,

First of all, biggest thanks to

➢ My brain, which despite many attacks of confusion and biryani craving, still managed to complete this journey.

Secondly, thanks to

➢ My heart, which kept shouting "pyaar, dosti aur democracy!" like a background DJ even when life gave low battery warnings.

Thirdly, officially and legally thanking:

➢ Aarushi Madam (Boss Lady of my Life) — Without you, my English would be even more murder-ful than current. Also, you taught me that love is not about perfect grammar... it's about perfect timing.

➢ Kabir "Shayar Photographer" Bhai — For clicking my worst angles and still calling it "artistic vision." Bro, your poetry sometimes more confusing than my English, but dil se mast!

➢ Meher (Tattoo with Attitude) — For teaching me that even broken things can become beautiful art. Also, for threatening to punch me whenever I acted extra.

➢ Rohan— For showing ki real men can be soft also, like Dairy Milk kept in pocket during Delhi summers.

- ➢ Simran Sunshine — For reminding all of us ki asli sweetness chocolate mein nahi, smile mein hoti hai.

- ➢ Zayan Jokes Factory — For turning every fight into a laughter competition. And yes, bro, you still owe me chai for that dare-night loss!

Also thanks to:

- ➢ Tauji, Chand Kaur Biji, Iqbal chacha — For showing that wisdom doesn't come from Wi- Fi, it comes from sitting together and saying "Beta, ek aur chai pii le."

- ➢ Judge Mishra Sir and Courtwaalon — Because even though law is serious business, sometimes a little Bollywood shayari can save humanity.

Special thanks to

- ➢ My "fans" on Twitter, who taught me: If you can't spell "election" properly, at least make sure your intention is correct.

Lastly, one ultimate thanks to:

- ➢ Chai.

  For being there.

  When no one else was.

Ending this acknowledgements with my own quotation:

"Life is like chai — sometimes kadak, sometimes pheeka, but always needed. So stir it, sip it, spill it... but never stop making it."

Yours untruly,

Rajeev Yadav (@ProudRajeev95)

www.ingramcontent.com/pod-product-compliance
Lightning Source LLC
Chambersburg PA
CBHW050308260626
47156CB00005B/1717